I0762274

ORRI

INTERGALACTIC SURROGACY AGENCY
BOOK THREE

TAYLOR NEPTUNE
JASPER THORNE

RESCUE

ORRI

I've been a warrior all my life. I've seen things no man — or alien — should have to see. And after so many years of battle, I thought I'd seen it all.

Turns out life still has a way of surprising you.

It was supposed to be a fairly straightforward mission. Rescue the kidnapped humans from the compound and take down their leader, Kovarx. All was going according to plan. Until I saw her.

Curled up in a grimy cell, clothes tattered and hair matted with sweat and blood, I saw her. There were others there, and a child, too, but the moment I saw the woman curled up on herself in the corner, my heart nearly leapt out of my chest.

I knew that smell. Every alpha did. But here? Now?

She was human. She was omega. And she was going into heat.

Talk about poor timing.

"Get the others," I grunt to my comrade. "I'll take the injured one."

"Understood." No complaints here. Good, because if any of them tried to take her, I don't know what I'd do. I tell myself I just want to make sure she's okay, but it's more than that.

It's the primal call of an alpha to an omega. I know the others must be feeling it too, but maybe it's less strong since Soren and Rathgar already have heart-mates. That leaves Ivar and me, and if Ivar tries to lay a finger on her, even our friendship won't save him.

She shivers and wails as I gather her into my arms. Poor thing — she can't even walk. Her leg is swollen and bruised around the knee. A break, most likely. I grimace. We've got to get her back to the med pods at the surrogacy center, and fast. Our field medics can only do so much, and I don't want anyone else touching her until I know she's all right.

Females are already incredibly precious and sought after on our world, but add to that the fact that she's human, *and* she's omega? The heat makes her incredibly vulnerable. And her scent will drive any alpha in a mile's radius mad with lust if I don't protect her.

Yeah. Protect. That's it.

She quiets down as I hold her steady in my arms, walking as fast as I can back toward my mount. My cock throbs in my trousers; my mind races with muddled desire, but I have to focus on the mission.

All of this is nothing but a normal biological response. I already had my chance at love…and lost it. Harsh memories flash back into my mind, unbidden. I won't let what happened to Zannah happen to anyone else, least of all this precious, delicate creature from Earth.

She's so soft, so light in my arms as I hoist her onto the back of my aki. She sways, still not totally conscious, and I swing up beside her to hold her steady. Grabbing the reins, I kick Alyx into gear, heading back toward the transport at full speed.

The soft leaves brush against our faces as we tear down the path. Alyx's hooves patter on the hard-packed dirt of the road as she bounds forward. Leaves and a few stray pebbles shoot into the air behind us, and all the while my hair blows wildly about my face, sticking to my sweaty skin after a moment before I brush it away. To say nothing of my passenger…

This woman isn't used to riding our animals, I can tell that much. Maybe it's because she's injured, maybe it's because she's in heat, or maybe it's just because she's a human and unused to our world, but her body bounces and wobbles on Alyx's back with the grace of a rag doll. I have to hold her even closer to keep her from falling off, and that pours even more of her delectable scent into my face, threatening to short circuit my senses and ruin everything we've worked so hard for.

Back to the center, I repeat to myself. Deep breaths in through my nose. Out through my mouth. Back to the center. Back to the center.

Pay no mind to the blushing beauty pressed up against your body, her curves and soft figure practically made to fit against your own. Or the fact that I'm hard as a rock, throbbing with need to conquer and claim her as my own. To fill her with my seed and see her large with my child.

I squeeze my eyes shut and shake my head. Focus. Focus. Gotta focus. What kind of alpha would I be if I abandoned an unarmed and vulnerable omega, especially one in heat? She needs medical attention.

Not…whatever my hormones wanted to give her.

That part of my life is over, I think with a frown. I had a mate once, long ago. She was it for me, and no one — not even this omega — can replace her in my heart.

I'll take her to the surrogate center, make sure she's patched up, and that will be that. End of story.

…If only life were so simple.

"ARE YOU ALL RIGHT? Anything hurt? Besides your ankle, that is." I'm trying to check her for injuries as we ride, but her heat and scent makes it hard to stay focused on the task at hand.

She lets out a sound that is somewhere between a grunt and a whine. I'm already cursing myself for how it makes my cock ache. How it makes me wonder what she would sound like in bed, with me looming over her as she's about to take my cock…

"Just…my leg," she grunts at last. Her breaths come fast and heavy, catching each time Alyx lurches under us. I wish there was a smoother way, but she's got to get to the transport first. They can take her to the center from there.

They. My mind flares with unexplainable ire at the thought. *I should be the one taking care of her.*

My nostrils flare. My hands clench on the reins and I look straight ahead, focusing on our destination and letting it fill my mind. Anything but…that. Anything but her.

I try to keep her busy with small talk on the ride back, but to be honest it is for my benefit just as much as it is for hers. She's exhausted, in shock, and in pain, so she doesn't say much. I don't blame her. I can't imagine what she's gone through, and to be going into heat on top of that?

It's no wonder she's a wreck.

I do learn one thing, however — her name. Isabella.

Even the word rolls off my tongue like the sweetest honey, making rational thought difficult. I've heard Soren and

Rathgar talk about what it's like to mate with an omega in heat, but to be honest I thought they were exaggerating. I had no idea it would be this… consuming. But there's another problem with this whole situation. Even if I wanted to claim her, I'm sure she's already spoken for. She has to be.

Where is her alpha? Surely she has one. The Intergalactic Surrogacy Agency doesn't let just anyone hitch a ride to Aesirheim. They have to be matched to a compatible alpha who has already paid. So what had happened?

"There you are!" Orvox rushes out of the center and meets us on the walkway. Her hair flies out behind her in nervous waves. I've never seen her look so serious. "Thank you for bringing her back, Orri. Help me get her settled and we'll take it from here."

A flash of possessiveness roars up in my chest. The primal, alpha part of me wants to tell her to get lost, that she has everything she needs right here. But I know that's not true, and I know from the swelling of her leg that she needs more medical attention than I can provide.

"I'm gonna help you down," I say to the exhausted beauty atop my ride. "Give me your hand."

Her eyes droop, and her ankle is already an ugly shade of purple. However, she's just aware enough to hear my words. As she leans forward, I catch a glimpse of her ample cleavage.

Even though I'm holding my breath, her aroma surrounds me; it's even stronger when her hand lands in mine. Good thing Orvox is about to take her off of my hands, because I feel my control wearing thin after the ride here.

I know she needs help. I know she's hurt. But some darker part of me doesn't care, and that instinct scares me. So with all the mental strength I can muster, I pull her closer and hope for the best.

Carefully, Orvox and I get Isabella down from my mount and onto the stretcher. No sooner is she laid down than Orvox is already connecting wires, running tests, and checking vitals. I couldn't leave her in better hands, no matter what my hormones are saying about claiming her and filling her with my offspring.

"Thank you again!" She calls over her shoulder as she pushes Isabella inside. I turn to leave, but at the last second Isabella lifts her head and I swear, she looked right at me.

That isn't the same terrified, glassy stare she fixed me with the entire way back. There's a fire there. A passion. She mouths the words before the doors swish shut and she's out of sight:

"Thank you."

AESIRHEIM, normally so vibrant with life and activity, goes silent. I stare at the doors for a long moment. My thoughts are still with the small, precious human inside. Alyx nudges me with her snout, but I give her an absent-minded pet and think no more of it.

I can still feel Isabella's heart beating against my chest. Her soft breath on my neck. I remember her warmth, so different to many of our females who run cold. When I think back to the condition I found her in, I'm amazed she managed to survive at all.

I don't know what she did to get under my skin like this. I've seen so much battle and hurt and pain, nothing fazes me. Usually. But whether it was her soft features, her shocked expression, or the supple warmth of her curves against my body, I can't bring myself to turn away. I have to know more about her.

Isabella.

The name rings in my head and rolls off my tongue.

Isabella.

My cock still aches at the thought of her scent. I shouldn't be as worried as I am. This facility is the safest place for her, especially during her heat. If she doesn't have an alpha, then...

I shake my head. Going down that path will only bring heartbreak.

I'm worried about her. That's it.

And not because the terrified helplessness on her face reminded me of

Zannah in her last moments, when I realized I couldn't save her…

When I realized the one promise I swore not to break went up in flames.

I make up my mind and lead Alyx to the stables. I'll stay nearby for now. Just to give Soren a progress report. He'll want to know. It's the professional thing to do.

And maybe by then, I can put this foolish notion out of my head.

MED-POD COFFIN

ISABELLA

Warmth. A spreading, burning warmth that envelops me from head to toe.

Itchiness. Like the scratchiest sweater everywhere and nowhere all at once.

Brightness. Blaring into my eyes, miles of white as far as the eye can see.

Those are the first three things I notice when I awaken.

I open my eyes to see the inside of one of the special med-pods they use here on Aesirheim. When I saw them for the first time at the center, they looked awfully claustrophobic. It made my skin crawl to think about being trapped in one of those things, like some kind of high-tech coffin.

I vowed at the time that I'd never go into one of those. At least, not willingly. But as my body rouses toward consciousness once more and I realize my predicament, I have to admit it's a lot more comfortable than it looked from the outside.

I could just be really high on whatever drugs they gave me.

I wiggle my fingers first. Then my toes. All still there. All attached. Some sort of warm gel envelops my lower body, and there are faint holographic readouts on the outside of the pod. My fingers twitch and come into contact with the gel. It covers my hand and moves up my arm, feeling like a warm, wet massage. All fear, all pain soaks away in its wake, and instead of panic, I feel peace.

This isn't so bad. It's like taking a hot bath back at home…but with alien massage slime instead of hot water and bath beads.

My vision sharpens; the gel retracts, leaving a trail of heat in its wake.

Oh. Right.

Heat.

The novelty of the med-pod and the strange slime almost made me forget about my 'little problem'. Almost. Suddenly I'm not so sure the wetness between my thighs is just from the warm slime anymore. My mind buzzes; my hole clenches around nothing.

Empty. So empty. And my only chance at relief gave his life to protect me.

I might be physically healed, but I'm pretty sure there's no cure for a broken heart. Or this gods-blasted heat.

Images of the raid still flash through my mind with violent clarity. Bjornick, my assigned alpha, taking up arms to defend me and our neighbors. Bjornick, overwhelmed and outnumbered. Bjornick, as his dismembered head landed at my feet and they came for me next…

I shudder, and even the sedative properties of the slime can't stop the searing pain in my chest.

We might have been good together, the two of us. After all, we were matched. Too bad I'll never know. We only had one week to get to know one another, and now he's gone. Whisked away like so much dust in the wind. I swallow the lump in my throat and float further into the drug-induced haze, wondering what could have been.

I signed up for the surrogate program as a last resort. I had an asshole of an ex-fiancé to escape from. When I realized the depth of his depravity, I knew I needed to get away. Far away.

Off-planet is about as far as you can get.

Yeah, I knew they'd pair me with an alpha and I'd have to have his child. However, if the stories I heard were true, it had to be better than taking my chances on Earth with Adik.

We didn't have to be soulmates or even lovers, but I needed the protection that the ISA and that Aesirheim could provide. The shot that should have triggered my heat clashed with my menstrual cycle — talk about bad timing — but I figured that meant I had more time to get to know the strange new alien alpha before we went to bed together.

That little delay had almost cost me everything.

In the week we'd spent together, he proved that he was everything my ex wasn't — kind, caring, and gentle. An utterly affectionate cinnamon roll who simply wanted to adore me and agreed that he didn't want to rush into anything physical. He wanted to wait for my heat to kick in fully as well, so we waited for the right time to conceive our child.

After we waited, the raiders came to ruin everything.

Bile churns in my stomach and threatens to come up. I need to sit up. I need to get out of here. But I can't move — not enough to unlatch this thing, anyway.

Wait a second. I can't move!

The beginnings of a panic attack start to take hold. Memories and sensations filter back in, reminding me just how very screwed I am. An urgent beep comes from somewhere outside the pod. That's probably not good.

Craning my head back and forth, I can't see a lot. My breaths come in short gasps that fog up the clear viewport and blur the world beyond. There aren't any other pods in here that I can tell, but there's a huge light above like what used to be in our dentist office on Earth. Its blinding glare gives me tunnel vision, and only through the corner of my eye do I see a door open and a figure walk in.

They're standing right next to the pod, tapping at something — maybe the controls? Then the beeping stops, and the lid of the pod whisks open, the slimy gel draining away.

"Oh, good." A voice says. All I can see is a stark silhouette. "You're healing up nicely."

Footsteps. Another voice, this time one I can recognize: Orvox, the head ambassador of the Intergalactic Surrogacy Agency. If she was here, that meant…

A new wave of fear washes over me. If my alpha — it feels so strange to call him that — was dead, what would happen to me now?

Would they send me back to Earth? Would they match me with a new male?

There's that rising panic again. I can't go back to Earth. I just can't. I'm a sitting duck down there. Good as dead. The police didn't seem to care. Adik was too much of a smooth talker and never left evidence for them to find. At least up here I have a chance.

And there's something else there, too. Something I did not notice before in the wake of the panic and confusion. A sweet, subtle scent that lingers just outside my periphery. The scent of an alpha.

It is not like the stagnant, rotting smells of the men that captured us. It's pine, cinnamon, and the starry sky on a clear summer night.

Visions of a different sort float through my consciousness, looking for an anchor. Strong, golden arms holding me against a wide, flat chest. Fierce eyes like embers, threatening retribution on my captors. Tenderness and caring as the compound and the kidnappers faded into the distance…

"Bjornick…?" I mutter, still half out of it.

I turn to one side and see the kindly face of Orvox blinking down at me.

No. Not Bjornick. Her.

"How are you feeling?" She asks, holding out a kind hand to help me up. I'm still bleary headed and the throbbing heat pounds between my legs, but I'm not in pain anymore. At least, not physical pain. Not of that kind, anyway.

"Um." There's too much on my mind to pick a single thing to focus on.

"You've been through a lot. It's all right." She helps me over to an exam table and pulls a blanket out of a nearby cabinet, handing it to me. It's a small gesture, but my fingers work their way through the chunky stitches and the softness comforts me. Too bad it can't come even close to wiping away the violent images that crop up every time I close my eyes.

"Thanks," I mumble, holding the blanket close. I'm hot and cold at the same time. Too alone and not alone enough. I need to be touched. No, I need to stay in my safe little shell and ride this out.

Ugh, who knew heat was so confusing?!

"Can I get you anything? Some water, perhaps?" Orvox has the same serene, motherly look she always does, but this time it's a little unnerving. The man who was supposed to protect me was murdered before my eyes. I was kidnapped, injured, and then subsequently rescued by yet another alien alpha. Then they stuck me in that med pod for who knew how long, and I was supposed to be *casually okay* with all of that?

"Water sounds good." My throat scratches and burns with each word. I have a million questions, and I'll need my voice to ask them.

But where do I even begin?

ONE CUP of electrolyte-infused water later, I'm feeling a bit more human, but just as confused as ever. Orvox is still talking, trying to explain something about the fine print in the ISA contract, but I can't focus no matter how hard I try. That stupid, lingering scent is still there, just out of reach.

I may as well just tell her to leave. All I want to do is be alone at this point. But then again, that's not totally the truth either.

What I really want is whoever has that delicious scent to take me to bed and fill me so thoroughly I can't walk…

To make me scream out until my voice breaks and there are no thoughts left, just wave after wave of ecstasy…

"Isabella? Are you listening?" Orvox's voice jolts me out of my fantasy. I blink and look up at her, mouth agape like an idiot.

"I, uh, zoned out for a moment there." I admit. "Sorry."

"You sure you're feeling all right?" She frowns, putting a hand to my forehead. "You can stay here as long as you need, you know."

"I'll be okay." My heart thunders in my chest with one goal and one goal only:

Get out of here. Find that smell. *Or that alpha.*

I'm about to ask her if she has anything to help with the heat symptoms, but then she says something I don't expect.

"What I was saying was, that male alpha that brought you here, he's still waiting outside. I don't know what he wants, but you know it's not safe for an omega in heat to be around an unmated alpha like him. I can make him leave, if you want."

"No!" The words tumble out far too hastily, before I even have time to process them. I take a breath, calming myself after seeing Orvox's shocked expression. "I mean, no. That's all right. I would like to thank him first."

I hop up off the exam table and wobble on my feet before righting myself. "For saving my life," I add.

Orvox moves toward the door like she is about to resist, but she stops herself. "If that is what you want," she says at last. "If you need help, you can always call using your communicator. We'll be right here."

I'm already out the door, but she's still calling after me. Something about stipulations and contracts, but that's not what matters right now.

I'm just trying to be nice. Gotta thank the guy that saved my life, after all. That's all it is.

Definitely not due to the hot, heady memories of his toned body against mine or the almost feral growls he used to menace the attackers.

Definitely not. Been there, done the whole 'gruff alpha' thing before back on Earth. I know that alphas are bad news. Not falling for it again.

…or so I hope.

SCENT

ISABELLA

I step outside into the fresh morning air. The sun barely rises above the horizon, and I realize just how long I've been out. I don't remember a lot, but I remember the sun being high in the sky when I arrived here. It's one of the last things I remembered before they carted me into the center and put me in the med pod.

That means close to a day has passed, or maybe even more. And that male alien was still out there, waiting for me?

The thought both confuses and excites me. I turn a corner out of the front entry to the stables and parking area, and that's when I see him clearly for the first time. Even reclining, he comes up to my midsection. Muscles on muscles cover his shining, metallic skin and the first rays of sunlight reflect off of it. I squint against the brightness, holding a hand up to my forehead.

His arms are crossed and head bowed. Sleeping? He was out here all night? The creature he lays against is even more incredible — an 'aki', if I remember correctly from some of the other girls talking about them. The closest thing I can compare it to is a giant elk from Earth, but even that's not quite it.

I've only been on this planet a short time, but the environments and the creatures never fail to astound me. From the luminescent mushroom forests to the wild beasts with antlers taller than I am, it seems like everything is bigger on Aesirheim.

Hmm, I can't help but think in my heat-induced stupor. *Everything?*

Not that I wanted to find out.

He looks up the minute I come into view, and his eyes latch onto mine instantly. I freeze for a moment, caught by his ferocious intensity. Even after just waking, his entire being exudes power. Presence.

A small, primal part of myself screams *threat, threat, threat*! But a larger, even more consuming part draws me closer with every step I take. Every ragged breath and beat of my heart.

Alpha, alpha, alpha.

Breed, breed, breed!

I let out a shaky breath. Faintly I hear Orvox at my back, rushing out to bring the bag I left behind. But it's all so far away now. There's only him —

And that *scent*.

I grit my teeth. Clench my fists. I'm better than this. I can push through these stupid urges long enough to at least say thank you. Then I can hole up in my nest and take care of things the old fashioned way. No way was I gonna let some random alien alpha mount me just cause my hormones were going crazy.

Right?

The huge alien alpha stands, and he's even taller up close. I suck in a breath despite myself, the area between my thighs clenching in anticipation. I've never seen anyone so *big* in my life; even though I was pretty tall for a woman back on Earth, he utterly dwarfs me here on Aesirheim.

He takes a step forward, his gaze darkening. Then his attention shifts to something behind me. I don't have to look over my shoulder to know it's Orvox.

"All you all right, then?" His voice comes out too formal, too measured for his hulking frame. He clears his throat. "I promised Soren I would stay and check on you. He asked for a report."

"Oh." My face falls. So he was just following orders. Nothing to do with wanting to see me at all. I should have known that he didn't really care on his own. "I wanted to thank you." I can't help but avert my gaze. My cheeks flush as the memories flood back in. "For saving me, back there." I lift my head and catch his gaze, still as intense as ever. I pull my bottom lip between my teeth. "I never even got your name."

"Name's Orri." He shrugs, as if introducing himself isn't important to anyone. I'm glad to learn his name.

Orri. What an interesting alien name. I've never heard anything like it before. "Orri," I repeat, and I like the way it sounds.

"It's no big deal," he adds. "I was just doing my job."

It's a big deal to me, but his tone makes it clear he doesn't want to talk about it or want to encourage me to make something more of it than it really is. I try to change the subject, instead. "Um, are the others all right? I haven't seen anyone else since…" I wince, thinking of how brutal the attack had been and how violent rescue had similarly been.

"Yes, we were able to evacuate everyone safely. And don't worry, Janie has been reunited with her child as well."

Oh, good. Memories of the cell are still weak and hazy in my mind. However, I remember the tiny human girl, no more than a few years old, crying out when her mother was taken away. What kind of vile savage would kidnap and torture a small child? An involuntary shudder makes me curl in on myself, nausea fighting its way back up my esophagus.

"You do not need to worry about them anymore," he continues, as if he knows what I'm thinking. His voice is smooth and even like he's giving a briefing to one of his superiors. It's lost all the command and alpha-ness that haunted my drugged-out dreams. Maybe I was imagining the whole thing. Maybe it was all part of this stupid heat…

Right on cue, a lancing pain shoots through my abdomen, so fierce and crushing that I cry out and double over, right there in the dirt. What is happening to me? It's so much stronger, so much sharper than anything I've felt thus far. I knew enough from the pamphlets and talking to other omegas that heat was never particularly *comfortable,* but this sharp, shooting pain was something else entirely. It felt like a hot poker being jabbed into my gut, right over my womb. I never thought going into heat would hurt so much.

I groan and clamp a hand over the area. My vision blurs again. I hear shouting, both male and female, but I'm too weak to look up. Suddenly, the scent from before grows stronger once more. Warm, golden arms hold me steady, and the moment we touch the ache abates little by little. I blink open tear-flecked eyes and stare up at him, mouth agape.

Orri.

"Are you all right?" He asks again, his formal cadence all but forgotten. "What's wrong?"

Orvox is on us in an instant. "She's in heat, you fool. Her alpha passed during the raid, and she's going to be very unstable like this without medical attention. You shouldn't have to be around her like this. For both your sakes."

My heart roars in my ears. I can barely breathe. Barely move. I know Orvox has a point, but the thought of being put in a med pod again…

"No," I mumble, clinging closer to Orri's chest out of instinct. I can't explain it, but being next to him makes me feel…safe.

He makes the pain and burning go away, even just a little. I know he's not *my* alpha. And I know he probably has someone of his own. I could never impose…

But I want to. I really, really want to.

Orri seems to have other ideas. A growl rumbles deep in his chest and the vibrations echo through my skin all the way to my heart. Instead of feeling afraid, a sense of peace and contentment washes over me. That, and bone-tired exhaustion. My eyes droop and my limbs cling to him for dear life.

It's wrong in so many different ways, but I just want the pain to stop.

"Are you implying I would hurt the female?" Orri's voice cuts through the tension.

Orvox taps on my shoulder, trying to pry me away. "Let's go, Isabella. You can't stay here, it's not safe—"

"No!" I cry out before I can think. Before I can stop myself. I'm practically sobbing, clinging to Orri's chest and rubbing my face against his bare skin. So much for dignity. I need relief, and being here with him is the only thing that seems to help.

"Isabella, please." She peels me away with surprising strength, and the moment Orri and I stop touching, the pain comes back with a vengeance. I grunt and wrap both arms around my midsection, trying to make it go away. The world spins, and suddenly, he's there again. Strong arms. Warmth. Scent. Safety.

Alpha.

All I can do is cling to him on instinct. He's the only anchor I have right now, and I don't even know the man. I know only one thing for certain:

If they take me again, if they put me in one of those pods, I'm not going to make it.

CONSENT

ORRI

Fuck. Me.

This female is trying to kill me, I just know it.

She's clutching at me frantically, small omega body burning up with heat and hormones while she rubs her maddening scent over my chest, my hands, and my clothes. The soft, needful whimpers reach my ears and lodge deep in my chest, rousing something long dormant, ever since I lost Zannah. Something I thought I'd never feel again.

How am I supposed to resist an omega in heat? How am I supposed to be a good, upstanding alpha when she's throwing herself at me like this?

"Give me the girl," Orvox urges, crossing her arms. She's nowhere near my size or physical strength, but she has a presence all her own. We know not to mess with the agency — angering them would mean no more omegas for us and certain death of our people without any young.

But when she's this close to me? When she smells so *mine*?

Screw the bigger picture.

“No,” I growl. I lay a protective hand on the back of her neck to hold her still. Since when was dark human hair this soft? It sifts through my fingers like the finest sand, softer than the most luxurious silk. Her skin presses against mine, flushed and darkened with need.

My cock throbs and strains against my pants. Even my heart races at her closeness, breaths coming in shorter, hotter gasps as I hold her close.

“Orri, you know the rules.” She isn’t the type of woman to back down, but neither am I the kind of alpha who .

“Screw the rules,” I spit before I can stop myself. “Can’t you see that she’s suffering? She doesn’t need your claustrophobic med pods and random nurses poking at her all hours of the night. She needs an alpha. How did this even happen, anyway? Where is her alpha?"

"Dead." She finishes my sentence with cold, cruel finality. "Bjornick fell to the raiders."

My mouth drops open, and now it's my turn for a sudden, sharp pain to seize my chest. Zannah's horrified face flashes before my eyes, frozen in death. Zannah's last words to me before she passed out of this world forever.

"I'm sorry."

No. My mind's made up. I won't leave Isabella to her fate. Not again.

“Take me to her nest.” I command, hoping I look as serious as I feel. It’s too easy to scoop her up in my arms, her head lolling against my chest. She doesn’t even resist, just hugs me closer. Yeah, I need to get us alone. Now.

“Orri—“ Orvox says in warning.

“Don’t make me say it again.” I don’t care what kind of paperwork I have to fill out, how many boring meetings I have to sit through, how many slaps on the wrist I’ll get from Soren for this. I don’t care. Isabella is in pain, and it’s in my power to help her. To turn away at a time like this…

No, I vowed to never do that again.

“Take me. To. Her nest.” I bare my teeth and draw myself up to my full height. I wouldn't attack her — not really — but she needs to understand I'm not backing down. After few more tense moments, she relents, but I can tell she's not happy about it.

"Fine," she says at last. "But if I hear even the slightest rumor of trouble, Orri—"

"You won't. Let's get out of here. Now."

"I hope you know what you're doing," Orvox sighs, and then we're off.

* * *

THE WHOLE WAY back to Isabella's 'nest', my mind races with an agonizing combination of emotion and need. I remember all too well the way

I failed my previous mate, Zannah. Isabella is not my heart-mate; none of us are lucky enough to get two in a lifetime. However, that's all right. She doesn't need to be, at least for tonight.

I'm simply doing her a favor. I can't bear to see another woman, especially an omega, in pain. And maybe because she just lost her alpha, I can relate with her just a bit. I know nothing about this other male or the relationship he had with Isabella, and I definitely don't want to try to replace him. But the way Isabella sobs and whimpers and claws at my bare skin like I'm her last lifeline to sanity…

Gods have mercy.

Orvox is still behind us, talking about all the medical implications and things

I need to do to make sure she passes her first heat successfully. I'm only half listening, and that half is only because I know its important for Isabella's well-being.

I had no idea omegas had such a complex mating cycle. It was never like this before. We fought and fucked as man and woman, not alpha and omega. We got horny, sure, but it was nothing like this. This...heat, Orvox called it, was closer to a sickness. A dangerous one, at that.

If she didn't have sex with an alpha, the raging hormones could cause hallucinations, fevers, even full-body seizures in extreme cases. When she put it like that...it seemed almost cruel to subject someone, even a human stranger, to that.

However, that's why organizations like the ISA exist. That's why they have so many rules and structured steps to follow. Didn't mean that I had to like it, though.

And really, what was the alternative? Continue to have failed pregnancy after failed pregnancy with our own females? The psychological, emotional, and physical tolls on us as our unborn children died tore us apart. We could not have continued to ask our own females to undergo more of the same.

All of this was all because of that alpha serum us warriors took way back when. When the war was at its breaking point, we needed an edge. Something that would give us strength and power the enemy didn't — and couldn't — have.

We trained night and day, but it still wasn't enough. Fortunately, the scientists came up with something. An experimental new drug that would enhance the natural capabilities of our bodies. Make us bigger, stronger, faster.

I was one of the first cohort to take the shot. I was the youngest one in the group, too. The alpha serum turned the tides and helped us win the war, but…

The changes it caused in our bodies made us less compatible with our own women. We needed to find a solution, or our race would die out forever…

Hence, another drug was developed. The omega serum didn't seem to work on our own people, but it took marvelously in humans, making them extra fertile.

And extra horny, like Isabella here.

If I could relieve even a little bit of that pain, maybe all the battles and struggle I've gone through won't have been for nothing.

That's what I tell myself, anyway. Because the alternative — that I might actually have feelings for the girl — is unthinkable.

My heart will always belong to Zannah. No amount of hormones can change that. But for tonight, I will do my duty. I will protect this woman in need.

And it's not *all* altruism. Helping Isabella through her heat is something I'm doing out of kindness and concern, sure, but I'm still going to enjoy every second of it. I grin in anticipation.

HEAT

ISABELLA

Warm, fuzzy feelings surround me. And not the good kind, either. The sharp, stabbing pain subsides with each step Orri takes and I burrow deeper into his embrace, well past the point of thinking logically. His strong scent is clouding my mind.

Why did this have to happen to me? To me, of all people? I came to Aesirheim as a last resort. As a way to put my abusive ex behind me and start a new life for myself.

So why did I feel like I was the one being punished? Heat racks through me in unrelenting waves, leaving me panting and sweating and writhing in Orri's arms. I know I must look a mess, but I can't help myself. My body's moving on its own, and right now it wants — no, *needs* — the touch of an alpha.

Too bad this was exactly the type of thing I'd hoped to avoid with Bjornick. Hooking up with a random alien without any thought to how he would treat me as a person? That's part of the reason Bjornick and I wanted to wait and form bonds of affection before I became pregnant. He really was too good to me…

But with Orri carrying me fireman style, growling and stomping away from the scene while heat threatens my very sanity, it's kind of…attractive?

I try to remember Orvox's promises. That I don't have to do anything I'm uncomfortable with. That I can back out or call for help at any time.

But as much as I don't want to admit it, their type of 'help' isn't what I need right now. I need an alpha to hold me, treasure me, and breed me until I can't see straight. I need him to roar out my name as he pumps me full of load after load of hot, sticky cum.

I need to lose myself in the immeasurable pleasures only an alpha can bring to his omega, and dammit, I need it *now*.

Orri isn't my assigned mate, and he's definitely not my heart mate, but he will have to do until I can get through this heat. Because I'm definitely not going back in the med pod. It was creepy enough the first time, and gross slime that seemed to have a mind of its own? So not my jam.

Orri smells…right. I can't explain why it's instinctively perfect. In the swirling inferno of lust and fear, something about him calms me. He's my anchor in the storm, a lifeline when I need it most. If someone asked me what he smelled like, I don't know that I could even describe. It's a subtle combination of all my favorite things — chocolate, a crackling fireplace, and some spicy scent I can't place...

Wait, does this guy actually smell like a *s'more? With cinnamon graham crackers?*

That delirious thought is the last one that stays with me as my eyes droop closed and I nuzzle into the warmth of his neck, letting instinct take over.

He's here.

He's an alpha.

And he's going to make sure I'm okay.

WHEN I COME TO, I'm in my old cottage, the one I shared with Bjornick, I realize with a pang in my chest. Some of his old clothes are still there, draped over the back of the chair. I remember scolding him about it. It was all in good fun, of course. I told him an alpha needed to be more organized, and he told me he *was*, just in his own special way.

It was an endearing little quirk…and now even that was gone.

The sound of a growl wakes me completely, and I gasp, pulling the covers up around my chest. Memories of the last few days rush back in in an instant.

Bjornick is gone. I was in heat.

Oh, and this growly alpha was gonna 'help' me through it.

What a sacrifice, I think while rolling my eyes. Really taking one for the team. But my snark fades when I see him sniffing Bjornick's discarded sweater.

The growl that resonates from his chest is deeper than any sound I've ever heard. It rattles around in my chest and settles deep into my belly, the warmth there reaching inferno levels.

This isn't right to be lusting after some alien alpha I just met. But then again, isn't that what I signed up for? It was only through a quirk of timing that I had more time to get to know Bjornick, but somehow, that little miscalculation had brought me here, laying in bed with a hulking golden alien snarling at me.

"These clothes," he says with a scowl. "They reek."

Okay, so Bjornick wasn't the best-smelling alien, true, but…

"Just put them over—"

"No." It's a hard, cold word that leaves no room for argument. "I do not like smelling another male in your nest. Not while you're with me."

Oh. I open my mouth to retort, but find that I can't. My pussy contracts at his possessive words, and I'd be lying to say it didn't steal the breath right from my chest.

He *wants* me.

And, despite everything, I want him too.

"Get up." He strides to the bed and scowls at the blankets like they might bite. "Now."

Before I even have time to move, he gathers me in his arms and gently sets me in the plush chair before returning to the bed. With a single motion, he tears the sheets and blankets off of the bed, tossing them into a corner.

"What are you doing?" I ask when I finally find my voice. "How are we going to—"

Orri rounds on me, his demeanor savage but his touches are nothing but gentle. He eases me out of the chair, holding me close in a way that speaks to all of my omega urges. He leans down so that his lips brush the shell of my ear. I shiver at his boldness.

"If I'm going to take you, I will not do it with the smell of another male in *my* omega's nest."

I suck in a breath. *His* omega. I wasn't. Not really.

But when he said it like that?

Maybe I could be. At least for now.

My thoughts wander and I find myself thinking about Orri with another woman in his bed. Pleasuring her, whispering all the sweet nothings into her ears just as he had into mine.

To my surprise, it frightens me. No, more than that. It *enrages* me in a way I have never felt before.

A small growl of my own rips free before I can stop it. I didn't even know I could make those kinds of noises. But

Orri pushes all of my buttons, even the ones I didn't know I had before.

Heat crawls up my neck and centers on the point where his lips meet my ear. With a ragged sigh, I can't hold it back anymore. I melt into his touch, and whisper to him with just the same ferocity, "Then let's get started."

BREEDING INSTINCTS

ISABELLA

Orri paws at my body like an alien possessed, his huge, rough hands pulling clumsily at the buttons on my shirt. One pops off and bounces across the room with a *ping!* that's all too reminiscent of another ping, back on Earth…

My mind drifts, thoughts darkening as I remember Adik doing the same thing. He only cared about himself and acted like he had a right to me. To my body. He came home drunk one night and ripped at my shirt just like this.

My whole body tenses up and even through the haze of lust and heat, I start to retreat. My trauma is surfacing and ruining the moment. I won't go through that again. I won't…I can't…

"Isabella."

The sound of my name brings me out of my stupor. A warm, gentle hand cups the back of my head.

"Isabella."

The fog thins, but only slightly. A rough thumb brushes over my cheek and I realize he's wiping away a tear.

"Hey." His voice echoes through my body and grounds me to the present moment. "Stay with me. You're here now. You're okay." His other hand rubs between my shoulder blades and he leans down next to my ear again, letting my head rest on his strong shoulder. "I've got you."

Despite everything, he was being so... nice to me. I know I told myself I wasn't gonna fall for another alien alpha at the drop of a hat, but this side of him — the caring, protective nature that all alphas share — was honestly pretty hot.

And hot is what I am right now. Hot doesn't even begin to cover it, honestly. I'm sweating and shaking; my mind's going a million directions, trying not to think about the past but worrying about the present and afraid of the future and...

"Stop." It's a simple word, spoken with perfect clarity. In that single, precious moment, everything does stop for a fraction of a second. There's just me and him, the weight of his fierce, demanding eyes boring into my own.

I soften in his arms and he's there to hold me. Everything's still a bit murky, but I'm glad he's here with me. I can't imagine what it would be like to go through this alone.

It was supposed to be Bjornick...

But it's not, and now that he's dead and gone, it will never be.

"Listen to me, Isabella." Orri's grasp is gentle but commanding. "When you are here with me, I won't let anything happen to you. Focus on me. Before the night's up, you won't be able to think about anything but all the pleasure I'm going to give to you."

My pussy clenches at the thought, and before I can spiral again, he leans down to cover my lips with his own.

Orri is surprisingly sweet and tender. His full lips caress my own with warm, wet kisses. His tongue runs along the seam of my lips and I gasp at the spike of desire that shoots down my spine. He, of course, uses this opportunity to use his tongue even more — and that's when I realize that his tongue…isn't like a human tongue.

It's so much better.

His tongue flicks in and out of my mouth, exploring. With every thrust, his hips buck forward and I can feel his cock straining against his pants as it rubs against my stomach. I want to reach out and tear his pants off, but he's got me pinned to the bed. He controls how far I can go.

Orri's free hand goes under my ass and squeezes my plump, fleshy cheeks. I giggle a little and he grins against my skin. He pulls his tongue back and lets go of my ass so he can bite down on my lower lip. It's a small bite, a warning. No, a promise.

My panties are already soaked through, and I know he can smell my arousal thick and heavy in the air. It only makes my heat stronger still, washing over me in waves. My mind goes blank when he reaches down to cup me through my ruined panties. Even the contact through the fabric sends a jolt of friction straight to my clit; I grind into him.

Fuck.

"Let's get you to bed," Orri rumbles, and I can't help but agree.

Though the lust in his expression is nothing short of primal, he treats me with such delicate care I find myself in awe of the juxtaposition. Harsh and violent. Soft and charming. Are all alphas like this?

Bjornick was incredibly sweet, but, well...

"Look at me." Orri interrupts my thought. It's like he's reading my mind. Like he saw me drifting into the past. Gentle hands caress my face and shoulders. Ever so carefully, he lays me back on the bed, covered now only with one of the fresh linens from the dresser. My hair splays out around me, and as I lay there staring up at him, I don't feel threatened at all.

I actually feel wanted, and even though it's all because of the alpha and omega hormones, I'm going to hold on to this feeling for as long as I can.

"You're going to be okay," Orri assures me as he unbuttons my pants, gentler this time. He slips them down my legs and moves up to pull the half-unbuttoned shirt off my shoulders. This time I don't tense up, lifting my limbs to help him along. In a flash, I'm laying there in my underwear, and if the hungry gleam in his eye is any indication, that's not going to last long, either.

"You are so fucking beautiful," Orri growls, nuzzling his head between my breasts. His large hands run down my sides until they're gripping my wide hips. I've never been the skinniest girl, but Orri seems to revel in my softness. He digs his fingers into my curves and grinds his hard-on against my clit through my damp panties.

"Please, Orri," I whimper, arching my back. This maddening heat spirals further, coming to an inevitable crescendo, and if I don't have him in and on me *right now,* maybe I really will go crazy. I buck my hips up toward him wantonly, my breaths coming out in little gasps. "Please don't stop. Please don't make me wait anymore. Please..." I pant. "Alpha..."

That seems to do the trick. With a lustful growl, Orri rips the thin fabric of my panties straight though, leaving them discarded in shreds on the floor. My bra comes off next, and finally I'm bare before him. There's just one more thing.

My eyes widen as Orri shucks off his pants. The monster bulge that I saw from outside his pants doesn't do justice to the real monster within. Thick, veiny, and just as gold as the rest of him, Orri's cock stands at full mast. A shining bead of pre-come dribbles from the tip, and I can't think about anything but how badly I want to taste it. Taste him.

He moves from my lips to my throat, my collarbone, my chest. I arch my back when he gives each nipple a swipe of his rough tongue, but he keeps going lower. A strong hand spreads my thighs, and I'm wetter than I've ever been.

"Mmm," Orri does that rumbling thing in his chest again, and before I can react, he buries his face between my thighs. Instant, mind-breaking pleasure shoots up my spine as his talented tongue swirls my nub. He draws it into his mouth and sucks gently, continuing to flick at the tip. In the meantime, his fingers stretch my opening and gather my juices.

I throw my head back and moan, my mind finally blissfully blank. In the tsunami of sensations, there's no more room for worry or fear or grief. In the moment there's only me and him, and the rapturous pleasure we are creating together. Orri starts working his fingers in and out of me, curling upward just enough to hit —

And it hits all at once like a bolt of lightning. "Aaah, I'm gonna—fuck, Orri!" My pussy clenches and throbs around his invading digits, hips and spine bucking of their own accord. All I can hear are the sounds of his hungry growls, the wet sounds of his fingers plundering my cunt, and my own hoarse voice crying out for more.

Little by little, the world shifts and stabilizes. A portion — a tiny portion — of the urgent *need* is gone, but it's going to take a lot more than that. I groan at the overstimulation of his tongue still on my clit, gently pulling tapping on his shoulder. He looks up, face covered with my cum, and licks his lips. I've never seen a more satisfied look on a man.

"Need…" My mind's so blissed out from the orgasm, the words float just outside my awareness.

"I've got you," Orri promises me. "Can you roll over for me?"

That, I can do. I bonelessly roll over in bed, letting Orri move my limbs where he needs them. One hand bracing on my stomach and the other on my legs, he moves me onto my hands and knees. My legs quiver, still weak from the orgasm, but I know what's coming next.

I've had a mind-blowing orgasm, I'm wetter than Niagara Falls, and he's been stretching me with his fingers, but a momentary fear still remains when I look at the sheer girth of him:

Will it even fit?

“Never fear,” Orri says, again with that uncanny knack of knowing how I feel. “You were made for this. Your body will take my cock beautifully. Just remember to breathe, and let me know if anything hurts.”

“Okay.” I lean forward so my face is buried in the pillows and my ass is still in the air. “Just…please. I need…” I wiggle my butt at him, only one thought still remaining in my lust-crazed mind:

Breed. Breed. Breed.

A shadow passes over the bed as Orri’s huge form looms over me, and I feel the hot, heavy tip of his cock press against my folds. He sinks in little by little, stretching me far past beyond what I thought possible. To my surprise, it doesn't hurt. The stretch is more of a pressure, a tightness like a coiled spring. And I know that when I come again, all that pressure will release at once, echoing out through my body in tremor after tremor.

"Yessss," Orri draws out in a long sigh. "Fuck, that feels good." He runs a hand over the small of my back, his other still on my hips. "Are you all right?"

"Mhm," I moan, muffled, into the pillows.

"Good," Orri rasps, his voice taking on that primal edge once more. "You're going to want to hold on tight."

And with that, he pulls out and pushes into me, filling me impossibly in one fell swoop. It's nothing like the first thrust, which was an exploratory invasion, inch by inch.

This was a *claiming*.

The sheer force of it makes me cry out, hands fisting into the sheets while he uses my hips for leverage. Each thrust stokes the flames, but cools the burn. It's only a pleasant, comforting warmth now. My whole body simmers and tingles with something beyond just desire. I almost feel…safe? Is this how omegas always feel around an alpha?

But as his thrusts speed up and he's grunting and clawing and groaning, I can't think of anything else but him.

His cock. His hands. His voice is getting deeper and deeper, making my toes curl…

The tension breaks at last and my orgasm rushes through me, finally releasing all that built up desire and need. Wave after wave of clenching, throbbing pleasure races through me. Tears well up and fall, and I'm crying into the pillow because of the relief and how good it feels.

"Ah, shit, I'm gonna—!" Orri's body moves in tandem with mine, gripping tighter than ever, but just as he's about to come, he pulls out with a roar and I feel his release splattering over my sweaty back.

Wait. That doesn't fit. He was supposed to…

My formerly sated, comfortable omega instincts flare up. What was going on? Why didn't he finish inside of me?

Did he change his mind? Did I do something wrong?

I can't dwell on it too much in my current state, though. The burning ache of the heat has dissipated at last. My limbs are jelly, my hair wild and tangled. My skin is slick with sweat and cum, but right now, all I want to do is sleep. The stress and emotional high of recent events finally wears off, and I curl into him, closing my eyes.

LOATHING

ORRI

My hands clench the pure marble of the sink, knuckles as white as the tile. My haunted face stares back at me, almost mockingly.

In the other room, a beautiful omega is sleeping, and my cum's still all over her back. It's all I can do to keep from rushing back in there to take her again. Or to scoop up my seed and press it into her slit, making sure she was full of me and ready to make a baby.

This isn't like me. This isn't how it was supposed to go.

I thought I could control my impulses. I thought I could give her what she needed. But I couldn't even do that.

"She's not yours," I repeat, staring at myself in the mirror. "And I can't be hers."

But with each painful beat of my heart, everything in me screams to go back out there and make her mine. I can't. That's all there is to it. I thought I could, but I can't.

Not after Zannah.

Thoughts of her lovely face flash through my mind. Her sparkling silver eyes, so different from Isabella's dark orbs. The flush of her cheeks when she laughed. The quivers of her body when we lay together, and the soft, tender aftermath that followed.

Back then, I had everything I needed. Zannah was supposed to be my heart-mate, and everyone knew just how serious a bond like that could be. An alpha without his heart-mate could, at best, live out the rest of his days alone. At worst? He'd go mad from the loss and grief.

Was that what this was? I leaned over the basin and stared into my blown-out pupils, looking for an answer. I didn't even know anymore, and that scared me.

I forced my fists to my eyes and groaned. Clenching my teeth, I tried to slow my breathing and focus on Zannah. Focus on her scent. On her sounds. Of the promise I made to her as the life faded from her eyes…

"Dammit!" I curse as quietly as I can. I don't want to wake Isabella, but the storm of emotions raging in my heart right now are louder than the roar of a rocket leaving the planet.

Dragging in a shuddering breath through my nose, I let it out slowly and search for calm. I can do this. I'm an alpha, not some mindless animal. It's what we both need to stay unattached. That's *if* she even wanted me in the first place, which she doesn't.

Heat makes females say all kinds of crazy things.

And in some ways, she's in the same boat I am. She lost her alpha only days ago. I can still smell him all over the cottage, including the bedroom. I hate how angry that makes me. I hate the fierce impulses that drive through my being, begging to go back in there and cover her with my scent again and again.

I'm doing the right thing...aren't I?

I want to believe that, but why did sex with Isabella feel so much different than sex with Zannah? And why, whenever I try desperately to call Zannah's face to mind, to remember how she felt in the heights of passion, I see *her* face there instead?

I'm going mad. That's all there is to it. Turning on the faucet, I run my hands under the cold, bracing water and splash it onto my face. I pick up a washcloth and wipe myself down. Her scent is still all over me, invading my nose and taking up residence in my heart.

Maybe if I can just erase her scent…I scrub harder and harder until my skin's irritated and sore. It's no use. It's like she's sunk into my very being, and no amount of water or soap will wash her off.

As I toss the rag in the laundry basket and turn for the door, I catch sight of myself in the mirror again and can't stop myself from mulling over the situation.

Is this my punishment, then? For failing to protect Zannah? For letting my heart-mate die?

I close my eyes against the pain. I knew the day I lost her that I would grieve her loss for the rest of my life. I just didn't know it would be like *this*.

With a groan, I grab a fresh washcloth and head back out into the bedroom where she's still sleeping. Isabella looks so peaceful like this. So innocent. Her mouth parts slightly in sleep, eyes lidded and hair tousled. She's still naked and covered in my scent, and it takes everything I have not to wake her and tell her how I really feel.

I would only ruin her.

So, holding back my instincts as much as I can, I gently wipe down her sweaty, cum-covered skin. My touches last just a second too long, but I never said I was perfect.

At the end of the day, she deserves a real alpha. One who actually has a heart to give. I'll never be that alpha.

CORAL

ISABELLA

When I wake, I'm sore and alone. Pretty much what I expected, to be honest. The events of the last night are hazy at best, but I do know one thing.

I was in heat, nearly going insane from the force of it, and Orri…he helped me. Again.

Did this guy have a savior complex or something? First he rescued me from the kidnappers, then he personally took upon himself to watch over me during my heat.

Most of all, I remember how he loomed over me, all alpha and power and force, but still let me call the shots. Asked if I was all right. And only then did he give me what I wanted. What I needed.

I roll over in bed, realizing that I'm still naked, but there's a blanket around my shoulders and a pillow under my head. That must be his doing, too. My heart warms a little at the thought. Not in the painful burning way that my heat had, but a soft, gentle warmth that fills me from the inside out. Despite everything, it feels nice to be looked after and cared for.

I know Orri is definitely not my mate, and I'll probably be sent to someone else once they can find a match, but my mind still wanders. What would it be like to be with him for real? What kind of father would he be?

I shake my head at the ridiculousness. A sweet scent floats through the air, and immediately I recognize it as Orri's.

So he's still here.

I didn't expect that, to be honest. He could have done the ol' wham, bam, thank you ma'am, but he didn't. He stayed. And that said a lot about his character, whether we were assigned mates or not.

My heat is finally under control, but my pussy still aches from the night before. I'd never taken a dick that big, and near the end Orri wasn't exactly gentle. It was exactly what I'd needed, though, and I came harder than I ever have in my life. With that thought in mind, I flip the covers aside and slip out of bed, padding to the dresser when my bare foot steps on something hard.

With a pained hiss, I hop on one foot, looking down to find the offender. And just like that, my world shifts all over again.

I'm standing on the pier with Bjornick, looking out over the clearest sea I've ever seen. Waves of sea grass flow in the wind.

Little waves lapping at the shoreline with a calm, steady motion. An alien seagull calls out above us, and the smell of salt hangs in the air. It's a quiet, perfect moment.

I'm peering down into the crystal depths when I see something wash up on shore. It's a shiny violet color, as smooth as glass. Forked prongs stick out in all directions, sprouting out from a wide base. It might be sea junk to some people, but to me, it's beautiful.

Bjornick sees me looking, because of course he does. "Do you like it?" He asks, pointing. "That's coral all the way from the Shadow Sea. It's rare to see it wash up here."

I nod, simply enjoying listening to him talk. And before I can say anything else, he hops off the pier and onto the sand, picking up the piece of coral and handing it up to me. "For you," he says with a smile on his face. "Let's go home."

THE CORAL. The rare coral that Bjornick gifted me that day at the beach. We must have knocked it off the table last night in our haste. My chest seems to cave in on itself, the grief fresh and raw as I pick up the sharp object and hold it carefully in my hands.

But now it's not just grief. There's something else there that hurts almost as much, if not more.

Betrayal. Guilt.

I squeeze my eyes shut, already feeling tears welling up. What was I doing? Bjornick gave his life to protect me only days ago, and here I was hopping in bed with another man. Did he really mean so little to me?

Did this gift and all it represented mean so little?

My chest heaves and I rush for the bathroom, slamming the door closed before I let out a long, shuddering sob. Bjornick gave so much for me, and where was I? Leaving his gift, his promise on the floor while another man smeared me with his scent during a heat that should have been when Bjornick and I conceived our own child.

I should have known better. Maybe I should have gone back to the ISA and let them handle it in the med pod that had felt like a coffin after all. First losing Bjornick, and then this, and then an inevitable third male after they found me a suitable replacement…

Was this all there was for me? Constantly running, constantly hopping from one man to the next, never finding a place to belong?

Because that's what happened to me on Earth, too. That's how I ended up here in the first place. I lay the coral on the counter with shaking hands and it slides into the sink, resting there against the drain.

I dare not look at my distraught expression in the mirror. I know I look like a total mess after all I've been through the last few days. Attacked, kidnapped, injured, threatened, rescued, unconscious, mad with heat, and then last night, screaming out with more pleasure than I've ever known…

With a growl I step into the huge walk in shower and tug at the knobs. There's a million different dials, soaps, and lotions, but I don't care about finesse right now. I just want the biggest waterfall possible to wash away my pain. My grief. My sins.

Blasts of water pour out of every spout. Some of it's red hot, some of it's ice cold. A slippery drizzle of shampoo foams up and drips down from one of the nozzles near my head. There's so much going on, so many sensations at once, but at least it's something I can focus on other than my pain. I adjust the knobs till the temperature's bearable and stand there under the spray with my washcloth, letting the tears fall.

I scrub and scrub at my skin. Try to cleanse myself of the memories and the pain. But the harder I scrub, the more it seems to cling to me. To crop up in my memory, again and again.

Those men, grabbing at me and pulling me and laughing. Watching as Bjornick fell right before my eyes, his mouth open in a final plea for mercy. Their rough

hands and rougher threats as they led us far away and threw us into the cell. I'd tried to stand up for the others — they had a child, for god's sake — but they took it out on me instead. Slapped me right across the face, threw me down hard enough that I twisted my ankle and heard something crack as I fell onto the concrete.

Their lewd gestures. Their terrible threats that we'd be good for breeding, that they'd take turns with us until we weren't of 'any use' anymore. The cries. The whimpering. The fear. And on top of it all, the heat...

IT ALL WASHES over me like a tsunami, and I crumple under the pressure, sliding down the wet, soapy wall and curling in on myself, not caring that the water's still running.

It will wash away my tears, and I'll try to forget about losing Bjornick. Someday.

RAIN SHOWER

ISABELLA

The shower pours down on me like rain, the deluge mirroring my emotional state. I'm ugly crying on the shower floor, my limbs shaking and my mind on fire as every cruel moment flashes through my head over and over, fresh as it was the first time. I'm frozen in place, caught like a helpless deer in the headlights, and all I can do is sob. For all the things I've lost, and all the things that could have been.

I thought I had a chance to rebuild my life here on Aesirheim. I thought it would be a new start, a new beginning.

I thought a lot of things, and none of them came true.

So here I am, sobbing and alone in this high-tech shower. Guess money can't buy happiness after all. My mind drifts for a few moments as I drown (almost literally) in my sorrows, then the atmosphere changes slightly. The rush of moving air floats over my tired body, and then the shower spray suddenly stops. I open my eyes. Did something break?

No. Orri's there, right in front of me, crouching between the shower water and myself. He's still wearing a white shirt and something similar to boxers, but seems unfazed by the water. His gaze rests solely on me, and without a word, he reaches out and takes my sobbing body into his arms.

Confusion bubbles up first — I thought he'd changed his mind about me? — but the sheer need to be held wins out and I melt into his arms. I'm still sobbing, still shaking and clinging to the wet fabric of his white shirt. It's getting soaked and it sticks to his skin, going translucent and accentuating each of his muscles. He doesn't seem to care, just holds me closer. One hand finds the back of my head and brushes the wet strands away from my face.

I know he's saying something, but I'm caught in a whirlwind of fear and confusion. The deep timbre of his voice glides into my ear, his sincerity carrying the words even when I don't want to hear them. That doesn't matter though, when I can feel the warmth of his skin and the gentleness of his touch. One arm holds me to his body and shields me from the spray while the other deftly turns the knobs and lets it all drain away. Without another word, he gathers me up in his arms and stands, carrying me out of the shower and back into the bathroom itself.

Tears stream down my face, wetting his bare chest, but he doesn't let go. He doesn't leave, even when I'm slumped and sobbing against his shoulder.

He works with incredible, determined efficiency. That much I can recognize as he grabs my clothes and sits me on the bathroom counter, looking up at him. He flicks a switch on the wall next to the lights, and a heated fan starts blowing from above, covering us with warm air and drying our bodies. The warmth soothes my muscles and lulls me into a soft, gentle embrace. He doesn't let go of me the whole time, and though there's still a war in my mind, having him here next to me is the tether I need.

Feeling his strength and his presence isn't quite *enough,* but it soothes something deep inside of me and keeps the worst of the panic at bay. Visions and snippets of the past few days fly in and out of my mind still, but they float by and go on their way now, like leaves on a stream.

The years I spent with my abusive asshole ex Adik. The crazy gleam he got in his eye when I defied him, or when he had too much to drink. The long nights in secret while I researched the Intergalactic Surrogacy Agency, and finally found the right time to sneak out and catch a shuttle over to the center. The fear and trepidation I felt as I went through their intake procedures, wondering if this would really work.

And then the awe and hope that came over me as we touched down on Aesirheim, and the charm of my alpha mate being the most kind and gentle man I'd ever met. More than I deserved. To the flames of the raid. The fear. The sickening crack of my bones breaking on the concrete floor as men laughed and jeered at me.

Then there was Orri. Only Orri. He saved me. More than once, actually. He saved me from the kidnappers. He made sure I got medical assistance. And then, in the depths of my heat, he was there, all raw lust and power and snarling alpha.

Except for one thing. The thing I needed above everything else…

When we're both dry, he picks me up again and carries me to the bedroom, gathering several of the blankets in one arm while still holding me with the other. He's so strong, he makes multitasking look easy. We go into the living room, where he lays down several of the blankets and sits me on top of them on the couch, making sure to wrap every inch of my body in their swaddling warmth.

Mmm. I know it must look kind of silly, but the warmth and weight of the blankets quells a little bit more of the rising panic. It's nice, actually. Like a cocoon, protective and safe. He leaves the room for a few seconds, and a spike of fear crackles up my spine for an instant before he returns, this time without a shirt and wearing a clean and dry pair of shorts.

A few water droplets still cling to his toned body despite the dryers. My eyes follow one of them down as it rolls past his pecs and down the ridge of his abs before disappearing into his waistband. My mouth goes dry at the sight and my heart skips a beat, because those shorts leave nothing to the imagination.

But then he sits down next to me, wraps his arms around me, and just… sits there. Letting me feel his presence. Not demanding. Not expecting anything. Just being there.

And that's more than any man has ever done for me before. It's nice.

I sniff, the last of the tears drying on my cheeks. When I look up at him at last, his eyes are soft. Worried, even. This isn't the face of a man who's going to hurt me or betray me. He looks genuinely concerned.

Which is all the worse for me, because I shouldn't be wanting him in the first place. I shouldn't be feeling any of this at all, because Bjornick…

"Isabella." The word finally breaks through the mental fog when I see it fall from his lips. "You are safe."

Safe. Funny how for so long, that was something I took for granted. And yet it's something I haven't had the luxury to feel, not in a very long time. I blink up at him, my tear-reddened eyes burning. "I..." My throat burns. My voice cracks. "I shouldn't…Bjornick… if he was here…"

"He would want to make sure you were safe, and happy." Orri finishes my sentence. And it dawns on me that maybe he's right.

It doesn't change everything right away. And it doesn't take away the grief and loss I feel for Bjornick. But what if…accepting Orri's help was not a betrayal, but a sort of homage to all that we'd had?

"Don't worry." His words wash over me and little by little, I relax into his arms. "This is normal. You're okay. I've got you."

I focus on my breathing. In. Out. In. Out. I've been through so much. I'm so tired.

And is this the perfect way that I thought things would end up? No. But right now? The warm embrace of an alpha's arms is enough, and I let myself drift into a peaceful state of being, buoyed by his warm words.

"Listen. I know you don't know me, I know we're not 'official' or anything, but—" He stops, letting out a sigh. "But I'm not an asshole. I see someone hurting, I want to help. That's what it comes down to, and I'm not going to let anything happen to you." His hand brushes over my hair and my eyes flutter closed. "Just stay here and relax with me. I've got you."

My trials aren't over yet. I know that much for sure. But until I gather my strength again, Orri is my shelter from the storm.

ANOTHER TRY

ORRI

I've gotten myself into some pretty big messes in the past, but this one takes the cake. All I was trying to do was be nice. Help out an omega so clearly in need, especially when I was nearby and had both the time and capacity to do so.

Yeah. Being nice. That's all it was.

At first.

But as she trembles in my arms, tears leaking from her dark eyes and drying on her beautiful face, I've never felt more conflicted in my life. On the one hand, I know this is wrong. That I shouldn't be getting so close to such a young, pretty woman who could never be mine. Especially an omega still grieving her lost alpha. What kind of jerk would I be, to steal her from another man, even if he was already dead?

I'm an alpha, and that comes with a certain amount of possessiveness. But I'm not an asshole. Do I tense up at the smell of the other man? Do I wish it was me, in some forbidden part of myself, that she was attached to instead of Bjornick? Sure.

But that's just basic biology. A simple cause and effect reaction that has no emotional bearing. Or at least, that's what I keep telling myself. Maybe if I repeat it in my head enough times, I'll actually believe it.

My cock aches in my trousers, tenting the fabric between my legs. I grimace and try to adjust myself with one hand, glad that her eyes are closed. She deserves a nice, long rest, far away from the horrors of war and loss.

Too bad I can't have the same.

Every time I look at her soft, innocent face, I can't help but imagine tearing these blankets off and spearing her with my cock all over again. How badly I want to see the flush of her cheeks. The arch of her back. The rapturous sounds of my name on her lips.

But I didn't get to see any of that, because I'd so foolishly thought that taking her from behind meant I wouldn't get as attached. That I could simply pump into her, focus on the physical sensations, and give her what she needed to get through this heat. It was *just* sex to help her. Didn't have to mean anything other than that.

Oh, who was I kidding?

It took every scrap of willpower I had left not to spill in her tight, needy pussy. Not to breed her full of my cum the way she — no, the way we *both* — needed.

I scrubbed a hand over my face. Maybe, in another life, if things had been different…

I look past her still form and focus on the landscape outside the windows. Each tree and flower. Each cloud and each bird. I mentally catalog them all. It takes my mind off the immediate rush of feelings, but they're still there, simmering in the back of my mind. And before I can catch myself, I start to speak.

Softly. To myself more than to anyone else. But maybe she needs to hear this just as much as I do.

"We're not so different, you know."

Isabella doesn't answer, and I don't expect her to. She's probably sleeping, but I need to get this off my chest.

"I lost someone, too. Long ago." The aching feeling in my heart returns, not only for Zannah this time, but for Isabella and all she's been through recently. I know firsthand how it destroyed me to lose Zannah. And now I'm sitting here, comforting this scared, perfect creature caught up in the wrong place at the wrong time. She started off her life on Aesirheim with highly traumatic experiences.

"Life has a way of throwing us curve balls. Giving us answers we don't expect, and leaving it to us to figure out how to pick up the pieces." My hand runs absentmindedly through her hair, and her breathing slows.

"There was a girl. Zannah." Even saying her name brings a fresh ache to my chest. I've never talked about this with anyone, not even my closest comrades. But sitting here with her, the words tumble out like water through a damaged bucket. "We met when we were kids. We grew up together. She was strong, bold. Ambitious." A nostalgic smile crosses my face. "She wanted to train as a warrior, just like the rest of us. And she was good at it, too. Even beat some of our most talented fighters a couple times while sparring."

Outside, the wind steadily blows through the valley, sending waves of floating flower petals across the grasslands. They alone bear witness to my words.

"I had a crush on her since the first time I met her. As we grew up and became adults, I thought for sure she was the one for me. We did everything together. Fought together. Ate together. Trained together. After a while, we even moved in together."

For a while, the only sounds are the thudding of my heart and Isabella's soft, even breaths. Far away, in the kitchen perhaps, a clock imperceptibly ticks away the seconds.

"I thought we were in love. It *felt* like we were in love." I let out a breath and shake my head. "Perhaps I was blind. She never said as much, but I knew that we were meant to be together. That we would be heart-mates, if only she could see that it was time to bond together..."

The sky darkens further, and a clap of thunder sounds in the distance. Funny, then, that it matches my darkened mood exactly.

"I never got a chance to tell her how I really felt. And that day on the battlefield when she looked up at me, covered in blood, and told me to run..." My chest seizes up and my voice breaks. This time, tears fleck to my eyes instead. Damn it!

"I failed her." My voice cracks, shoulders shaking. I haven't let myself feel this much since she passed. I didn't think I'd ever find another soul I could open up to. But something about Isabella, even if she was sleeping and exhausted, made me feel safe for once in my life. Made me feel like perhaps I could change the ending of my story.

After Zannah's death, I'd come to terms long ago that I'd grow old alone and die alone, without a woman to warm my bed or claim my heart. But what if that didn't have to be the case?

I don't know what to think anymore, and I don't know how to put it into words. If I told all this to Isabella while she was awake, she'd probably look at me like I was completely crazy. Despite all appearances, I've never been too good with emotions. Turned them off and away, like most of us did. On the battlefield, they were a liability. And in our personal lives?

Too many of us had experienced loss there, too.

I run a hand softly through Isabella's dark hair again, letting the soft strands fall through my fingertips. She won't ever be mine, not in that way. But she doesn't have to be. For the time that we have together, I'll do my best to be the alpha she deserves. If I had been the one to fall that day, leaving Zannah alone without a mate, I would hope someone would look after her.

Would take that precious girl into their arms and bring a smile back to her pretty face. So that's what I'll do. Stay by her side, be the rock she needs.

And at the end of it all, we can both part ways knowing that we did the right thing.

The sound of a sniffle catches my attention and when I refocus on the scene in front of me, Isabella's awake. And looking right at me. I freeze.

How much did she hear?

And why was she crying?

"I…" She starts, voice warbling. "I had no idea, Orri. I'm so sorry." She wraps her arms around me and shifts even closer, laying her head against my chest.

She heard it. She was awake, possibly even the whole time.

And I just spilled my deepest, darkest secrets.

What have I done?

"It…" I struggle to find the words. The emotions that so eloquently poured out of me only seconds ago stutter and stop, suddenly unsure. I didn't mean to say all of that stuff in the first place, but once I got going I couldn't stop…

"It was a long time ago."

"Still," Isabella says. She reaches out and takes one of my hands, linking my fingers with her own. I marvel at the size difference, her hand small and doll-like in my own. The soft touch moves me more than all the sex we had. For a moment, we're no longer alpha and omega, or even man and woman.

Just two people, sharing a similar pain and taking comfort in one another's presence. That's the word for it, I realize at last. There's lust there, sure. There's possessiveness. But on top of it all, there's a sense of peace and safety and *comfort* I feel with Isabella, and I've never felt that with anyone.

Not even — I realize with a shock — with Zannah.

What does that make me, then? *Who* does that make me? I don't have the answers, but for right now? Just staying like this in her presence is enough.

"I know you lost a mate, too," I start. "And I know how fresh it is. How painful. I remember how much losing Zannah hurt me. How much it still hurts me, when I least expect it. So I don't want you to think I'm trying to replace him, or that I'm trying to say he doesn't matter." I take our joined hands and bring them to my lips, kissing her small, soft fingers. I don't know why, it just feels right.

“I honor and respect this alpha Bjornick for everything he did for you. For all of us. He died an honorable death protecting the ones he loved.” I pause, letting the lump in my throat pass. “Just as Zannah did.”

A few moments of silence pass, and Isabella’s the next to speak. “So where does that leave us?”

I look deep into her tender brown eyes, and see something there that looks suspiciously like hope.

“Isabella,” I say, making sure she hears the conviction in my voice. “I will do my best not to feel shame or guilt during your heat, for however long this—“ I gesture around us, “—lasts. We’ve both lost someone, and we both could use the companionship. But I want you to promise me something."

"What's that?" Her eyes are wide, her lips parted, and I've never seen anything so beautiful.

"That you'll do the same for me."

I watch as her throat bobs with the weight of her decision. She sniffs one final time, swiping away the tears with the back of her hand. Isabella gives me a squeeze, and that little touch holds the promise of so much more. "I'll try."

And just like that, something shifts between us. There's still so much work to be done. Still so much baggage to unpack. But the icy outer shell cracks at last, and I feel myself aching for her all over again.

Apparently I'm not the only one, because she lets out a low, breathy sigh while pawing at my chest. "Orri, I'm sorry, I know it's not the time, but…" She looks up at me, sweat beading on her forehead and eyes wide with need. "It's coming again, the heat, and I don't think I can…"

"Shhh. There's nothing to apologize for." I cut her off with a kiss and lay her out on the couch. It had hurt me to hear her cry the last time. This time, I'm going to do this right.

GIFT

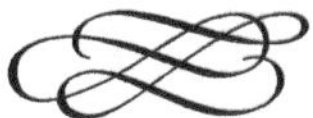

ORRI

The uncertainty still lingers in the back of my mind. The fear and guilt that maybe I'm making a mistake. That it wasn't supposed to be like this. But as I spread Isabella out on the cushions and peel each layer of blankets away from her trembling body, all I can focus on are her soft sighs and needful whines.

Fuck. And here I thought the last time it was hard to control myself.

If anything, she's even more needy this time, the initial resistance having worn off. Neither of us wants to drag emotions into this, but our bodies mesh so well together, and after sharing a moment like that, it only seems right. I press more kisses to her lips and face before moving to her ears and down to her neck.

She makes the most delicious squeal and jerks against me, the friction of our skin ramping my pleasure up even further. She has to know what she's doing to me. Well, I'm going to give it back to her in turn. Plus interest.

Isabella lets out a long, shuddered moan, using the back of one hand to cover her face. Gently, I take her hand in mine and pull it away. "There's no need to hide," I say. "I'm right here."

"I know," Isabella whispers, "it's just…"

"Shhh…" I whisper back, bringing her hand up to my lips. "There's no shame in how you are feeling right now. No dishonor. This is simply a part of who you are, and by honoring that, you're honoring all those who have come before you. Even Bjornick." A low, soothing rumble echoes out from deep within my chest, and I hope she can feel it. "Even Zannah."

Her eyes shine with emotion, and her hand relaxes, dropping to the pillows beside her head. With an even deeper blush, she nods her head, and pulls me in for another kiss. The need is so strong that I can barely control myself, but I hold back as long as I can. I want to savor this moment.

“I want you,” she says between kisses, and I almost groan at the words. Instead, I get on my knees, pull her hips into the air, and let my lips take over, my tongue and teeth soon finding the sensitive skin of her thighs.

I can feel her breathing grow more and more ragged. With every kiss, nibble, and lick, I draw closer to the place she needs me most.

"P-please," Isabella pants, making my raging cock even more rock-hard.

"Hmm. This?" And with that, I bury my face between her legs. My long tongue swipes around and across her sensitive bud and her back arches off the couch with a cry. I can't help but let out a little chuckle. "Or this?" I dip my face lower to plunge into her wet cunt.

Fuck, I forgot how good she tastes. It's like the finest, duskiest wine laced with pure sin. I lick and taste every inch of her, groaning in delight as her slick fills my mouth.

Isabella's whimpers of pleasure fill the air, as well as her scent, her arousal, her need. I can't hold myself back any more. Diving back in with gusto, I use my hands to spread her, licking, sucking, and fucking her until she cries out in orgasm.

With Isabella panting and trembling around my fingers and tongue, everything else from my past fades into the background. There's only me and her, and the sweet scent of her heat infusing everything.

Her breasts bob with every touch. Her skin flushes the prettiest shade of pink, and her moans — I could listen to them all day. I try to commit each curve to memory. To fix into my brain the way she says my name, or the blissful radiance she exudes when reaching that ultimate peak. Because no matter how fun this might be for now, that's all it's ever going to be.

For now.

Two hurt souls finding solace in one another.

For now.

I bring her close again and again, drawing back before we reach that peak. I can't help myself, her twitches and bucks against me are just so cute. So needy.

So *mine*.

"Please," she's panting, sweat rolling off her forehead. "Please, Orri. Please…"

I raise an eyebrow, looking up at her with my cum-covered face. "Please what?"

"F-fuck me. Please. I need y-your…" She trails off, covering her face with her hands again.

Though her embarrassed expression is nothing short of adorable, I'm not deterred. Gently, I move her hands away from her face. "My what? Tell me what you need, and you shall have it. I promise."

Her eyes, still rimmed with tears, sparkle in the glow of the ambient light. Or maybe that's just my imagination. Either way, this is a magical moment. Her whole body shivers beneath me when she says, no louder than a whisper, "your c-cum. Your seed. Please, Orri, I'm so empty, I need it, fill me up, please please *please*—"

Something snaps within me, and it's no longer a question. I have to possess her. I have to give her everything.

With a growl, I gather her to me, layering hot, needy kisses on her neck and shoulders while I line up my throbbing dick with her hole. She's so fucking wet, and when I slide inside, we both let out a long, guttural groan.

It's not supposed to feel this *right,* is it? This safe, like this is where I'm supposed to be? Like this is what I'm made for?

I don't have time to dwell on those kind of questions, though, because I have an omega in heat beneath me. And I'm going to show her just how an alpha pleases an omega.

This isn't the first time we've had sex, but doing it this way fills me up in so much stronger a way. Before it was purely a physical, mechanical action. An in and out, back and forth designed to reach a goal as quickly and as efficiently as possible. But holding her here in my arms, being able to look into her face as I thrust into her, awakens something deep in my heart I thought died long ago.

Every time I pull out her walls clasp around me, begging me not to go. She wails and clings to me with surprising force, and as my thrusts get longer and deeper, so too do my grunts. She seems to love that, though, giving back just as much passion and enjoyment as I'm giving her, winding us both up impossibly tight until we're teetering on the point of no return…

A split-second decision flashes through my mind: do I pull out again? I'm not supposed to come in her. I'm not supposed to get her pregnant.

Only an assigned mate from the ISA can do that. That was the deal.

I grit my teeth and clench my abdominal muscles as my balls draw up tight to my body. I'm close, so close. With a cry I pull back, ready to paint her skin with my cum again like I did the last time, but then Isabella does something I don't expect:

She lets out a cry of her own and her legs lift up to wrap around my waist, locking her ankles and pulling me back in. "No!" She pants, her eyes wild. "In me, in me, please, Orri—"

And the feel of her spasming pussy is too much to take — the last sliver of resistance fades away and I let loose. Stream after stream of hot cum explodes out of me, filling her up as deep as I can. The feeling is unlike any other and triggers something primal inside of me, something possessive and dominant and so very *alpha* it scares even me.

"Yes!" I roar, pushing in as deep as I possibly can. Fuck the ISA. Fuck the rules. She's going to take every last drop of my cum — because that's what she needs. That's what she deserves. An alpha who can fulfill even her most base desires and soothe the raging storm inside her.

As we lay there, entwined and panting, I realize something that tilts my world on its axis. What I did — what *we* just did — I'd never felt anything like that before. Not even with Zannah. And that scares me more than it should.

I don't know what to make of it, but I do know one thing.

I made two vows to Zannah long ago. One of them was to hold her in my heart and to never love another. And the other? To protect her from harm.

When she fell in battle, I was powerless to do anything about it. I failed my most solemn vow, and all I have left is the last promise I made to her. Even in death, she still has my heart.

And Isabella — no matter how good she feels or how *right* this all seems, deep in my heart — she's not ready for another man, either. She's still grieving, and I'm not going to cut that short for my own selfish desires.

I know there's nothing wrong with what we did. And I know it helped us both blow off some steam. I feel closer to her than ever after we shared our pasts, but there's one thing that hasn't changed.

I may give her my body, but I can't afford to give her my heart.

TRAINING

ISABELLA

At long last, my heat seems to be subsiding. And not a moment too soon, either. The ladies, human and alien, all told me that going through a heat would take a lot out of me, but I never realized just how much. Turns out being maddeningly horny twenty four seven is actually pretty exhausting.

Even if the sex was spectacular. I smile to myself when I remember the nights we've shared in bed. It's not quite the same as I expected it to be with Bjornick, but that doesn't make it bad. Orri is quite the skilled lover, much as it makes me blush to admit it. He had put me in positions I never considered before. He's able to read what I want with only a glance and sends me flying higher than I ever have before.

If I didn't know better, I would try to stay with him. See if I could work out a deal with the Intergalactic Surrogacy Agency. Just this once. But that's never going to happen. Not for him, and not for me.

With a sigh, I stretch out in the huge, luxurious bathtub, letting the scented water soothe away my tired muscles. I was never much for baths before, but I soon learned there's nothing better for a tired, achy omega. The water is able to reach places it just can't in the shower, and laying in the bath as the water surrounds me is like a warm, comforting hug.

That, and this is no ordinary bathtub. It's almost like a small pool, to be honest. I can sit down and stretch out my arms and legs without touching the sides. My head just barely rests on the edge of the tub, letting the water fill all the way up to my neck. And my favorite part? The jets lining the sloping walls of the tub, bringing much needed pressure to those sore spots.

My fingers slip down my sudsy body and come to rest over my stomach before I even know what I'm doing.

We've had sex a few times since that fateful night, but he only came in me the once. And I haven't been having any symptoms, so it's quite possible I won't get pregnant.

We came up with a compromise after that first night. Or should I say, he did. He went out to the store and came back with these alien-size condoms that would put a magnum to shame. They make me laugh, and they come in all kinds of fun textures that heighten the experience in the bedroom, but I'd be lying if I said that some small part of me didn't want him to bareback me again.

I want to feel the hot, tight skin of his dick as he thrusts it into me. I want the full, leaking feeling of taking his cum. Even if I don't get pregnant. The ISA says that's only possible with genetic matches, anyway. That's why the organization exists in the first place. The alpha mutation in the Aesirheim aliens makes them, or should I say their sperm, verrrry picky when it comes to finding a suitable womb.

Even an omega in heat sometimes isn't enough. It has to be a match not only emotionally, but also physically. To tell you the truth, my eyes glazed over during a lot of the information sessions I sat there at the ISA headquarters. I had much more pressing things on my mind at the time.

Like getting off-world as soon as possible to escape my no-good ex Adik.

But that's all behind me now. I'm millions of miles away on an alien planet. He can't hurt me anymore.

So why do I still feel so vulnerable? I wrap my arms around myself and stand, grabbing the fluffy robe hanging on the stand next to the tub. Even it's the height of luxury, the soft fabric clinging to my every curve keeps me warm and cozy as I step out of the bathroom.

The bed's actually made for the first time since coming here. All those other times, we were too possessed by heat to care about the sheets and blankets. It's a good sign that I was able to focus enough to make the bed this time. Means that at last, the heat's finally dissipating. Maybe I can go back to some semblance of a normal life now.

Ha, normal. My life is anything but.

I think back to last night. I tossed and turned in the king sized bed, the mattress and fluffy pillows feeling more suffocating than comfortable. Every other night, Orri had slept by my side. I told myself it was just because we were both so exhausted, but as I lay there staring at the ceiling, unable to sleep, I wondered if there was more to it.

I shake my head. No, I had just gotten used to his presence, that's all. And Orri must have noticed, too, because he came to my room in the middle of the night, complaining about the very same thing.

I'd be a fool to think it meant anything other than a platonic gesture. Just two lost souls helping each other out when they needed it most.

But would it be so bad to be his? My hand floats to my stomach again. To bear his child?

Gulping, I shake my head again. No sense in following that train of thought. It won't happen. Can't happen.

Not after Bjornick. And not after Zannah. My heart aches when I remember the story he told me. How he'd lost someone dear to him as well, and how he never really stopped loving her.

Even if I did care for Orri in that way, we could never truly be together. Both of us still had our hearts set on another, and it wouldn't be fair to either of us unless we had our full heart to give.

My throat closes up with the emotion of it all. But I'm trying to get back to a 'normal' daily schedule, as much as I can anyway. Bjornick's loss is still fresh in my chest, but there's another piece sitting there now, too. Orri, his warmth and strength and vulnerability.

There's nothing I can do about it, though. So I take a deep breath and step outside the cottage, hoping that some fresh air will do me good.

The moment I step outside, I'm hit with the same familiar scent that has surrounded me for the last week. Orri's here. And he's close.

I sniff the air again and a curl of warmth trickles down my spine before settling between my legs. I came out here to get fresh air, but it looks like I'll be getting anything but.

Before I can think better of it, my legs start moving and I follow the scent, curious to see what Orri's up to.

I hear the sounds before I see them. A rhythmic, metallic clanging, over and over. There's grunting, too. The sounds of exertion mix with the clangs and as I draw closer, his scent fills me even more strongly.

When I come to a clearing, I see what he's been up to. A wooden dummy stands before him, notched and battered with age and years of practice drills. Orri, unaware of my presence, swings his sword to and fro, hitting first the backside of the dummy, then the front. He moves with a fluid grace I wouldn't expect from someone his size, but he makes it look easy.

I watch for a moment longer before revealing myself. His muscles work and flex under the strain, each flex and strike perfectly timed and executed. Sweat rolls down his bare back, shining in the day's light. My mouth waters at the sight. So much for clearing my head.

The more I watch his complementary grace and power, the more I realize just how alpha he really is. It's one thing to take the name. There are a few dozen alphas on the planet, marked by the fact that they'd all undergone genetic experiments in order to protect their planet during a war.

Even so, talk is one thing. Action is quite another. And as I stand there, transfixed by his movements, my hand drifts for the third time that day down to my belly. Unbidden thoughts flood into my mind before I can stop them. They play in my mind one frame at a time like a photo reel, and the implications leave me reeling.

Orri, using those strong arms to lift a laughing child high in the air.

Me, round with child and positively glowing.

Orri, holding a tiny hand as they walk along the beach together and pick up shells.

And there's me again. I'm in the frame with them, wearing a sunhat and carrying a wicker basket to store their finds.

It's a nice vision. An idea of what life could be like, perhaps, if things had been different. But my stomach twists in on itself when I snap back to reality. There would be no fairytale ending for me. That ship sailed long ago.

Orri seems to finish up his drills, because he walks over to a bench, panting, before grabbing a cloth to wipe down the edge of his sword with some sort of oil. He sheathes it carefully and is about to leave when I can't take it anymore.

I had planned to stay hidden, but I couldn't let him leave. I didn't know why, just that I didn't want him to go. Not just yet.

"Orri!" I call out, stepping out of my hiding space and into the clearing.

He turns toward me at once, his lips quirking up in a grin. "I was wondering when you were gonna come out."

I open my mouth, then close it. He knew? The whole time, he knew?

"How long..."

"Ever since you arrived." Orri shrugs, as if it's the most obvious thing in the world. "Your scent isn't exactly hard to miss." He rounds on me, his eyes seeming to flare when they stare down into my own. "Especially for an alpha."

My breath catches in my throat, and suddenly I'm at a loss for words. Every idea flies out the window and I'm left standing there gaping like some kind of drowning fish.

He lets out a short laugh. "Heh. But besides all that, what brings you out here? I was just doing some morning warm-ups. Soren gets on our ass if we don't keep up with training, so I try to get in a few rounds whenever I can."

For the briefest second, the sight of grubby, pawing hands dragging me away from my home surface in my mind once more. But I push them away with a shake of my head. Because it's given me an idea.

"Can you...teach me?"

DRILLS

ORRI

I don't know what foolish thought possessed me to say yes to her request. She didn't know what she was asking. Not really. Otherwise she would never have said such words so innocently. So casually.

Ever since I was a child, ever since I could barely walk, I had been training to be the warrior I am today. Endless drills. Late nights. Early mornings. Sore muscles.

Sweat, blood, and tears.

Not to mention all of the field experience. All the men I'd watched die.

Zannah.

I wince at the thought, the same way I do every time I think of her. But for some reason, it doesn't have quite the same sting it once did. It's still there, of course, but it's like expecting a burn and finding only a comforting warmth.

Strange.

I don't have long to dwell on that thought, however, because Isabella's right there next to me, practicing the movements I showed her and looking up at me with a childlike hope in her eyes.

Fuck. She's too pure for the likes of me. She's hurt and been hurt so much already. She'd never go for a guy like me.

"How'd I do?" Isabella's cheeks are flushed and she's panting. A slight sheen of sweat shines on her forehead, not unlike the way she looks when we...

"Good," I mutter quickly. All too quickly. "Very good. You're learning fast." I only hope she doesn't hear how distracted I am. How much torture this actually is for me.

I have no problem with women warriors. After all, Zannah was one. But with Isabella, every alpha instinct I have screams to protect her. To keep her from harm's way at all costs, not to teach her how to fend off danger without me.

Without me.

That's a punch in the gut, but it's the truth. Once this little experiment of ours is over, we'll go back to our own homes, our own lives. That's the way it had to be.

Even if I lay awake at night cursing my very being for wanting to fill her with my cum so full that she'll never leave, so that she'll bear me many, many children...

"...hands-on." Isabella says something, and I only catch the tail end of it.

Busted.

"Huh?" Now I'm the one stuttering. "Sorry, I didn't quite catch that."

"I said, I'm tired of doing these poses. I want to try something more hands-on."

The sheer fire and determination in her eyes unnerves me. I gulp.

Yup. This girl was trying to kill me.

GRAPPLING with Isabella in order to teach her how to escape a predator's hold has to be either the dumbest idea I've ever had in my life...

Or the smartest.

She's not as strong as an Aesir warrior, of course, but she packs a surprising punch for a human. Her ferocity far exceeds her size, and I have to admit, I'm impressed.

But there's not a lot of time for thinking when your arms and legs are wrapped around the most delicious smelling omega you've met in years...

Isabella pants and strains against my hold, surprising me as she twists her thin wrist away with a torquing motion I can't catch.

"Ha!" She laughs, and for one surreal moment, the sight of her looming over me, grinning triumphantly, is the hottest thing I've ever seen.

I want to see more. I want to bring out that side of her. Two sides were already fighting a war in my head, but seeing this fire in her eyes makes it all the more difficult.

I want to protect her.

No, that's not quite it. Otherwise I wouldn't be rolling on the ground, snarling and pawing at her as she slips out of my hold.

I want to shield her from anyone or anything that may harm her.

That's not it either. I want to teach and pass on my techniques, so that she may grow and protect herself in the future.

It's a normal part of teaching someone. It's normal and natural to want to pass on one's skills. Nothing weird about that. And if there were going to be more attacks — oh, I hoped not —

then training the others in basic defense techniques might not be such a bad idea.

Another thought surfaces. It's not the others I'm worried about. Thinking about rolling around in the dirt with any of the other women — or men for that matter — does nothing for me.

But with Isabella, I feel something I haven't felt since...

"Ha, give up yet?" Isabella's straddling me with a smirk on her face, and even though we're both clothed I can already feel my cock hardening beneath my pants. Just a little bit of fabric in the way, and I could be filling her to the brim all over again.

No. Focus.

She leans forward, planting her hands on either side of my head. The silhouette of her hair against the sun brings out a beautiful halo, and when I stare at her flushed face and soft pants of exertion, I do something I haven't done since meeting her.

Make the first move.

My hands shoot out from my sides and knock her off balance. She gasps and falls forward, but I'm there to catch her. I pull her to me and embrace her with a kiss. It tastes like starlight and and sunrise all at the same time.

Like a tiny sliver of sun, trying desperately to break through the clouds...

As she melts into me and I kiss her back, again and again, I ask myself why that is.

Dammit, she feels *right.*

This wasn't supposed to happen. But how can I deny the way my heart beats when I'm around her? How can I overlook the very feeling in my soul that lights up when we touch?

I nip at her bottom lip and she lets out a little moan before pulling away. She's dangerous.

Just the kind of danger I can't get enough of, apparently.

With a growl, I roll us over so that now I'm the one straddling her. She looks so beautiful like this, hair splayed out around her and cheeks ruddy and skin marred with dirt and scratches. We're both covered in sweat and even I'm starting to take deeper, heavier breaths.

That's when I realize something about Isabella that I hadn't noticed before. The easy way she smiles up at me. The half-lidded look of peace, of satisfaction — no matter what I did or how much I tried to be a good partner — that's something I never saw on Zannah's face.

Not once.

The realization hits me all at once like a punch to the gut. Had I simply been deluding myself, all this time? Thinking that Zannah and I would be together forever, when it was only me who felt that strongly about her? I don't know, and I don't think I want to know.

I do know that if I give in now, all those years in mourning will have been for nothing. I know we promised each other we would try to get through this with as little shame as possible, but I'm learning just how hard that is. Easier said than done, that's for sure.

I do like Isabella. A lot. And not just because she's an omega and I'm an alpha. But I also still love Zannah. I love what we had together, even if it wasn't the perfect relationship. And I'll never get over the grief and guilt I feel over losing her.

It's not possible to have more than one heart-mate. It's just not. Everyone knows that. So either Zannah wasn't really my mate at all, or...

I grimace. I can't let myself think like that. It would undo all these years of grieving. All these years punishing myself, and for what?

I'm not ready to face the answers yet. I can't. So I jerk up. Try to pretend everything's normal. I hold out a hand to help Isabella off the ground, and by some miracle I'm not shaking.

I ignore her look of confusion. I don't say a word. Simply turn back to the task at hand. It's the only thing I know I can count on. It's the only thing that makes sense anymore. I can't fall in love with anybody, especially a human omega.

SOMEONE BETTER

ISABELLA

A FEW DAYS LATER

I let out a breath as I stretch both of my arms above my head. One leg is stretched out behind me, while I balance precariously on the other. My core aches, but I'm almost done, just a few more seconds...

"Aaah." With a relieved sigh, I right myself and loosen my neck, rolling it back and forth. Every morning since the 'training' with Orri, I've been doing some of the stretches and poses he recommended. I don't know exactly how they would help me defend myself, but he says everyone needs a good foundation. If these stretches help me build my muscles and stamina, then it's a win in my book.

Grabbing the towel I brought with me, I wipe the sweat from my forehead and head for the bathroom, in desperate need of a shower.

I've been trying to keep myself busy now that my heat is over. Trying to focus on my exercises and watching over baby Ray while her parents ran errands. But even when Orri's not here, I still find myself thinking of him.

Still find myself aching for him.

It's stupid. He's not even my mate.

But I can't lie to myself anymore. When I think of Orri leaving, or Orri with another woman...

I don't like it. I don't like it at all.

Whatever is going on between us, I don't want it to end.

He's grumpy and caring and rough and gentle in all the right ways, and he makes me feel things I thought I never could. The sex was great, of course, but it's so much more than that. The way he holds me at night when I can't sleep. The determined look in his eye the day he rescued me from the compound.

The inner struggle I see in his eyes every time he catches me looking.

This has all gotten so complicated so fast, and I don't know what to do. I talked to Lara briefly before returning to the cottage, and she told me she went through something similar. She did say, however, that if I truly cared for him, I need to tell him.

Holding it inside will lead to regrets, and after the pasts both Orri and I have had, we can't afford any more of those.

So that's it. I've got to confront him about all this. I've got to tell him how I feel. And I've got to hope that he doesn't dump me completely because of it.

The sound of movement distracts me and I wobble on my feet, losing my balance just enough until...

A strong hand catches me, the warmth steady and reassuring.

I look up at him, lips parted, mind racing. How long had he been there?

"It's only fair," Orri smirks. "You snuck around and watched me training. Why don't I get the same privilege?"

"That's—"

"Different? How so?" His eyes gleam with mischief as he releases me, and I notice that he's wearing his uniform again. It's the same garb he wore when he rescued me. I remember that much. My stomach sinks. Is he going out on a mission again?

A strange cramping starts deep down in my gut, swirling with unease. Even the thought of him leaving makes me feel ill. And I hate that I've fallen for him this hard, but here we are.

"You've improved, you know." Orri says.

"Oh." I didn't expect that. Thought he was coming in here to tell me he was leaving on a mission or something.

"I'll be honest, I wasn't sure about teaching you, but you've picked up on the fundamentals remarkably quickly." He pauses. "For a human."

Bam. Another cramp. More insistent this time. A strange lightheadedness crawls up my spine. Maybe I overexerted myself. Or maybe I'm just getting too worked up over all of this.

A moment hangs between us. I want to tell him. I want to have this conversation. But now?

Now.

"We need to talk." To my surprise, it's Orri that broaches the subject. "Being that your heat is over, and I still have my duties to attend to, I..."

Right. Duties. He's just going to leave me and pretend like none of this ever happened. Sure wish I could.

I try to think of something to say. Anything. But all of my carefully planned speeches vanish in the heat of the moment. "You're leaving." It's not a question. Just a statement. A cold recognition of the facts. And it's all that comes out.

"I have to."

Ouch. I can't bear to look at Orri's face. I stare at a spot on the floor and try to keep the tears at bay. "Did our time together mean nothing to you?" It's harsh, but it's how I feel.

I don't expect him to answer. I just needed to get it off my chest. He could just turn and leave right now, for all the good it would do. He's already made his position quite clear.

My stomach cramps again, just to emphasize that.

"It did." When he speaks again, his voice is hoarse. Different than the confident, commanding voice I've gotten so used to. "It does. I enjoyed every moment I spent with you, Isabella. You know that. Or I thought you did."

"So you're just going to run off now, like nothing's happened? Since I'm not in heat I'm not your responsibility anymore, is that it?" The emotions come on hot and heavy now, one after the other. I know I should take a step back and think before I speak, but all the frustration and fear and longing have finally come to a head.

"No, it's just..." He trails off.

"I've fallen for you." The words tumble out at a whisper, falling as quietly as the tears from my eyes.

This time I really do expect him to leave. It would almost be easier if he did. I don't want to hear his excuses. I just want him gone.

"Isabella..." The sound of my name on his lips is like a knife to my heart. "I'm not your mate...the ISA will find someone for you. Someone better..."

"I don't want—!" But the burst of emotion sends me over the edge and the lightheadedness reaches my face until everything's fading, my legs are wobbling...

"Isabella!" Orri calls out, rushing forward to steady me.

I can do that just fine on my own, thanks. I move to the couch and land heavily, putting my head between my knees and trying to breathe. The tears are still falling. My stomach's still cramping.

And my heart is still breaking.

I can still feel him hovering over me. "What's wrong? Let me help."

But I'm still too hurt to think clearly. "I don't want your 'help'," I say miserably, without lifting my head. "You've helped enough. Just go back to your life, Orri. You don't have to pretend for me anymore."

"Isabella..."

"Get out."

"Wait, we can—"

"GET OUT!" I yell, and without another word, he turns and leaves. I think for a moment he's going to resist, to come up with some reason to stay or call me out for disrespecting him and raising my voice. But he doesn't.

The door clicks, and so clicks closed any hope I ever had for a happily ever after. The world spins around me, and I lose myself in the uncontrollable sobs shaking my whole body.

VIOLENCE

ORRI

Blood. I guess that's all I'll ever be good for. All I can ever contribute to this world.

Just terrible, wanton violence.

I rip into yet another creature, watching as its innards spray the ground.

Blood and battle are all I have. All I've ever had, even when I hit rock bottom.

And if this isn't it, it feels pretty damn close.

It's been a week since I left Isabella in tears. It tore me apart to do so, but I knew I could never be the mate she needed and deserved. It lodged straight into my heart when she said she'd fallen for me. Haunted me in the middle of the night, so much that I wake up panting, pawing at the sheets for someone who's not there.

But this is how it has to be. Those are the rules.

After all, I'm nothing but a warrior. Guess I was never meant to have a happy ending.

"ORRI, WE NEED TO TALK." It's Ulfar, Zannah's brother. He remained on the team when she passed, and he's turned into a great hunter. Sometimes his mannerisms remind me of her.

"About what." I scowl into my drink, knocking back the rest of the dregs and wiping my mouth with the back of my hand. "We did our job, didn't we? What more is there?"

"That's not what I'm talking about." Ulfar's voice is stern, serious. "I'm talking about your behavior in the field today."

But that doesn't make sense. I haven't done anything wrong. I've fulfilled every task and every duty he set out for me. More than that, even.

"What about it?" I'm still looking for an exit, trying to remain as disinterested as possible. I don't want to talk about it, especially with Zannah's brother. I've been avoiding talking beyond what was necessary to him ever since she died. How could I possibly tell him what was going through my head? How would he ever understand?

Ulfar pulls up a chair next to me. I guess I'm not getting out of this one. "Listen, man. Since when do you have a death wish? I haven't seen you like this since..." He trails off.

"I don't want to talk about it," I grumble. Why can't he get the hint?

Ulfar's gaze flicks to the blade sitting by my side. Specifically, to the blue ribbon tied around the hilt.

Dammit. Should have packed up first.

"All right. All right." Ulfar isn't giving up so easily. "It's a female problem, isn't it? I know that look when I see one."

"Fuck off."

"Then why is her smell still all over you?" He nods at the blade. "And on that ribbon? What's going on, Orri?"

I let out a long, slow breath. Close my eyes. Of course he'd notice the damn ribbon. I didn't even notice it for a couple days after returning to my quarters. Somehow one of Isabella's hair ribbons — or maybe the sash to a dress? Had gotten mixed in with my clothing, and I didn't have the heart to return it to her. She made it clear she never wanted to see me again.

So what was the harm in keeping it? Of having a little something to remember her by?

Besides, her scent calms me. Even when I wake up in the middle of the night, panicking and thinking that something's happened to her, if I can just reach her scent, my body relaxes enough to go back to sleep. It's embarrassing as hell, and no way am I gonna tell Ulfar about all *that,* so I opt for a different approach:

"I was doing a favor for the ISA. I helped an omega through her heat after her mate died in that raid. That's really all there is to tell."

Ulfar scoffs. He's not buying that either. "Sure. So you're telling me you spent the last few weeks fucking the daylights out of an *omega,* of all things, and you're still this wound up? Man, I would say you need to get laid, but clearly that didn't help. At all."

I round on him, suddenly ablaze with emotion. "I would think you of all people would understand!" My hands ball into fists. My voice breaks. "I loved your sister, Ulfar. I wanted to spend the rest of my life with her. And that was stolen from me, because I couldn't keep my promise. I couldn't protect her when she needed it most. Now here I am whoring myself out to some random female just to feel something again...I don't know what's wrong with me." I bury my face in my hands and let out a groan. "If she was here..."

"If she was here," Ulfar finishes, and his tone is crystal clear, leaving no room for argument. "Then she'd tell you what a fool you're being."

The words hit me like a slap to the face. "How dare you—" My heart's in my throat and fuck it, I don't care if he's my superior, he's gonna pay for that.

"I know my sister, Orri!" His authority looms over me, as if saying 'try me.' "I spent a lot longer with her than you did. You don't think I know my own blood?" His eyes meet mine, and I have to admit that he is right.

I huff out a breath, and after a few heated moments, reason wins out. Maybe I *have* been blind all this time.

"There's something I need to tell you," Ulfar says. "Something I should have told you a long time ago. I mourned Zannah in my own way, and it didn't feel proper at the time, but..." He shook his head, grimacing. "She came to me, once. Talking about you. Not long before she passed, actually." He rubs the back of his neck and looks away, but presses on. "You thought she was your heart-mate, right?"

A heavy stone of dread drops into my heart and doesn't leave. My mouth goes dry. It's something I always suspected in the darkest regions of my heart, but never wanted to admit...

"She wasn't, Orri." The words seem to echo forever until they fill up every void. "She wasn't your heart-mate. She didn't know how to tell you." He swallows, then puts a hand on my shoulder. "I'm sorry."

Zannah wasn't my heart-mate. The carefully constructed worldview I had, everything I stood for, shatters in an instant. Everything I did — or didn't do, in the case of Isabella — was to honor Zannah's memory and the once-in-a-lifetime connection we had.

Correction: connection I *thought* we had.

I really was a fool.

"I'm sorry to have to tell you like this," Ulfar says again, and it actually sounds like he means it. "But no one else was going to." He stretches his arms over his head, leaning back in the chair. "It's tough being an alpha sometimes, huh?

No one ever wants to call you out when you're wrong."

Wrong. The word tastes so foreign on my lips. My feelings for Zannah were real, but the fantasy of us being heart-mates, of being together forever...

It was only that. A fantasy. And if that was true, then...

"Zannah wouldn't want you to throw away your chance at happiness," Ulfar says, and for the first time, I almost believe him. "And you know as well as I do, she'd be the first person to smack you upside the head for thinking that you were insulting her by finding someone else."

I don't know what to say. My mouth opens and closes, but no words come out. It's like everything inside me's being torn apart and put back together at the same time.

"I know you loved Zannah very much," Ulfar continues. "So did I. And I still miss her every damn day. But she's gone, Orri. As much as it hurts to hear that, she's gone. And it's up to us to make the best life we can. Living in a way that she would be proud of."

I guess I never really thought about it that way. Could I really let go of so many years of grief and guilt? It wouldn't be easy. But when I think about Isabella's smile, or the way she looked at me when she confessed her feelings...

Maybe I have it in me to try.

"This girl," Ulfar says after a long moment. "Do you care for her? Truly?"

That's a loaded question if I ever heard one. But with clear eyes I now see the truth. "Yes. I do."

Ulfar gives me a knowing smile. "Then you know what you have to do." He gets up, but not before giving me another reassuring pat on the back. "It's okay to let her go, Orri. It's time to live your life." And with that, he turns and walks away, leaving the door open behind him.

I sit there for a few moments longer, contemplating over my empty glass. Now that no one's here to see, tears spring up at the edges of my eyes. Everything I thought I had. Everything I thought I stood for.

With a sniff, I drew myself up onto my feet.

It was time to turn over a new leaf.

And that would start by winning Isabella back. I had to tell her how I felt, once and for all. ISA match or not. Because I can't bear to live another life full of regrets.

NEW ARRIVAL

ISABELLA

I'm fine. Really, I'm fine.

My heart's broken into a million pieces — again — but hey, who's counting? It's not like this is the first time I've been stuck in a situation like this. I'll put on a happy face and smile for everyone else. It's what they expect.

After too many nights crying and talking with the other girls, I've made up my mind. I can't stay here. There's too many memories. Too much hurt. And having to see...him...on a day-to-day basis makes me want to puke.

I've had a few more dizzy spells, but nothing as serious as that first one. I chalk it up to stress and the fact that I haven't felt like eating much. I'm sure it's nothing to worry about. Besides, I had panic attacks back on Earth, too. Maybe that's all this is.

Whatever the reason, I'm back at the agency, trying to hold back tears and pleading with Orvox to get me off this planet.

"There have to be other races, other matches, correct? It doesn't have to be here on Aesirheim?" The more desperate words only ring in my head.

Anything. Anything will do. Anywhere but here.

"It's certainly possible, but it is unusual..." Orvox frowns, looking me up and down. "And we'd need to run a full battery of tests of course, to make sure you're healthy enough for discharge. You've already been given the omega serum here."

I'm hardly listening, just nodding along. "Fine. I just...I can't do this anymore."

Orvox, for her part, isn't judgmental or nosy. She has that sense of eerie mother-like authority, and it makes me feel safe. "You're not the first to have gotten cold feet," she says, tapping away at her tablet. "I can re-route you, if that's what you truly wish, but you'll have to return to Earth to await re-assignment. Will you be all right with that?"

Earth. I tense up for a moment, thinking of the man I literally left Earth to escape. Adik - an abusive, worthless excuse for a man who wanted to own me and control me like a doll instead of a person. I shudder. "And what happens after that?" I ask, just to keep the conversation going.

"There's a transport coming in shortly, so you're in luck. A few traders and a new shipment of omegas will be disembarking, and you'll be able to catch a ride on the return trip today if you like."

Today. So soon. Am I really ready to make this kind of decision?

To leave behind this world — these people — who have become like family to me? I squeeze my eyes shut, trying to block out all the pain.

Earth didn't work out. Aesirheim didn't work out. Third times the charm?

"You don't have to decide right this moment," Orvox assures me. "But here's what we'll do. I'll take your blood sample now, and you can go get packed. Then meet me at the space dock and pending your test results, I'll sign the release for you to get on the shuttle back to Earth. Deal?"

I swallow the lump in my throat. It's incredibly generous. More than I deserve, really. But I still feel like something is missing. Something just out of reach, that I can't put my finger on.

"Come here, dear." Orvox extends her spindly arms in a surprisingly warm gesture. "You've been through so much. I only wish we could have gotten there sooner." She trails off, lost in some thought of her own. I sniff away the building tears and step into Orvox's embrace. Her skin is strangely cold and smooth, a contrast to the man-shaped furnaces their males turn out to be. Still, it's the care behind it that counts. With such a powerful alien holding me like this, I can almost believe that I'll be all right.

"Now, let me just get your blood sample, then I'll let you go pack. If you change your mind, you can call me at any time. Remember that." She draws away, a sad smile on her face. "I wish you all the best, Isabella."

"Thanks." And I do mean it. She's been more supportive than most of the people in my life have, but that's not saying a lot. And even though it will hurt to say goodbye to her and the friends I've made here on Aesirheim, maybe it's for the best to start over. I can wipe the slate clean again. I ignore the pain in my heart.

PACKING DOESN'T TAKE LONG. It's not like I brought a lot of stuff with me to begin with, seeing how I was trying to sneak off-planet as soon as possible to escape my toxic ex. I feared what he might do if he ever found out what I'd done. Going back to Earth came with its own set of fears and challenges, but Orvox assured me that I'd be staying in the center until I could be reassigned. Their security was top-notch, she promised, and it could be as little as two or three days before they found a new match for me.

Not a lot of time for things to go wrong. That's what I tried to remind myself, anyway.

I take the last shirt out of the drawer and something clatters to the floor. I bend down to pick it up and my heart thuds a little harder. The coral that Bjornick picked for me from our trip to the beach. And I see something else, too. Sticking out from under the dresser, just barely visible. A corner of white fabric.

Curious, I pull on it. Out comes one of Orri's tunics. Wrinkled and a bit dusty, but still saturated with his scent. My mouth drops open. How did this get there? It must have gotten pushed under the dresser and he'd forgotten it when he...

My heart sinks. My stomach cramps. When he left.

I stare at the garment for a few long moments. Almost hoping that it holds the answers I so desperately seek. But the shirt is just a shirt, at the end of the day. And if it has any secrets to tell, it's not giving them up to me. I sigh and look around nervously. There's no one else in the house, but just in case...

I bring the fabric to my nose and sniff, letting it fill my senses one last time. I remember his strength and his softness. His confidence and his caring. The way he held me when I cried. The way he gripped me so tightly, needfully, almost –

But then I remember the way he looked at me when I told him I was in love with him. The hurt behind those eyes. And the way he looked as he walked out that door for the last time.

Tears fall and splatter onto the fabric. With a huff, I ball it up and stuff it into the suitcase along with the coral piece. One memento from Bjornick. One from Orri.

Two men I'll never forget, for two very different reasons. And two reminders of what could have been.

So with a sigh, I hoist the suitcase upright and roll it to the door, leaving that life behind me.

* * *

I'M CHECKING my comm as I walk, trying to pull up directions to the spaceport and make sure I'm not running late. Orvox said she would meet me there and give me the final clearance to get in the shuttle back to Earth.

My stomach sinks even at the thought. Was it really worth going all the way back to Earth, to await yet another uncertain future? Yet another mate I had no say in?

Wasn't like I had much of a choice. A chill passes down my spine as I approach the busy spaceport. People, ships, and transports come and go, the hub a mighty nerve center of activity for the whole planet. I'm trying to read the monitor when I see movement out of the corner of my eye. I lunge at the last moment away from a speeding hover bike, its driver cursing at me in a high pitched voice. Sheesh.

After stepping out of the road, I peer up at the monitor again, trying to read the foreign symbols. I've learned some of them, but it's still a bit fuzzy to my eyes. Then I see a word I recognize:

Earth.

There's a green box with some text next to it, and the green box is flashing. Is that good? I turn when I hear the hissing of the hydraulic doors and there it is, coming in for a landing.

The sight of the shuttle to Earth brings back memories of my first trip up here. Oh, how things have changed since then. When I first came to Aesirheim on that very shuttle, I was scared, desperate, and alone. All I wanted was a way out. A second chance away from the controlling asshole Adik that made my life hell in more ways than one.

I felt like I'd never be free. Like he'd always catch me, no matter where I went. And if he ever found me, he made it clear in no uncertain terms what would happen...

I can't hold back a shudder as the memories flash through my head all over again. I'd done what I came here to do. Adik would never find me up here. But if I were back on Earth, even if it was at the surrogate center, there was a chance...

More hissing and the sound of metal sliding against metal as the ship hooks into its bay. I scan the surrounding platforms, looking for Orvox's tall, spindly form. I don't see her yet, so I decide to get closer. Besides when I arrived here myself, I've never seen a spaceship this up close before. And watching it land from the outside, instead of as a passenger, was fascinating all on its own.

The dock comes alive around the landing vessel, workers scurrying to and fro to set up the bridge and open the doors for the passengers. Down below, yet more workers check for signs of damage and hook up ports on the hull to the charging stations beneath the dock, allowing the ship to refuel and power up its auxiliary systems as well.

I'm so busy watching the workers maintaining the ship that I don't notice immediately when people start filing out of the ship and onto the bridge connecting the shuttle to the main walkways. Uniformed aliens of Aesir gold, a few young human women, a few more smartly-dressed businessmen of both human and non-human descent. There's even a green-skinned alien among the bunch — his skin a dusky emerald in contrast to Aesirheim's gold. But its the last person out of the shuttle that makes my mouth drop open. That throws me straight back into my own personal nightmare.

It's him. I don't know why or how he ended up here, but it's him. The ex-fiancé I fled the planet to escape.

Adik.

SURVIVAL

ISABELLA

This can't be happening. The world sways around me; my vision narrows to the scarred, hulking man lumbering off the bridge. My brain screams at me to run, but fear has me rooted to the spot.

My mind is short-circuiting, not knowing what to make of this new development. How did he get here? How did he know?

I thought I did everything right. I covered my tracks so well, and I figured if he was going to find me, he would have done so already. Why now?

As soon as I can consciously react, I duck behind a ticket booth, but it's simply too late. He has already spotted me.

Again, I scan the crowds for any sign of Orvox. I've seen her stand up to way scarier guys than Adik. She could vouch for me. But she's nowhere to be found.

I squeeze my eyes shut and try to breathe to calm myself down. Try to remember what Orri taught me about self defense. But it all flies right out the window the moment I feel Adik's callused hand grab me.

"Found you," he snarls, yanking me out of my hiding place. "Thought you could run from me, huh?"

I think about screaming. Wonder if anyone would understand or care if I tried to get their attention. But everyone's so lost in their own world, going back and forth with their own business...would anyone even notice?

My heart thuds double-time and adrenaline floods my system. Fight or flight kicks in and I try to yank my arm away, but he only holds it tighter. My brain throws those options out and goes for a third one. *Submit.*

But I can't — no, won't! Submit to him. He's the reason I even joined the ISA in the first place. He shouldn't be here.

He shouldn't have been able to find me. And now that he has, he'll...

"What's wrong, sweetheart?" His voice drips with malice and a sickening amount of triumph. "Not happy to see me?"

"Get lost." It comes out as more of a weak whisper without any power behind it.

"What's that? Seems like you're the lost one here." He taunts me further. Adik starts walking, but doesn't let go of my wrist. I'm forced to stumble after him, taking us further and further away from the ship, the crowds, and my only remaining salvation.

After we're out of the most heavily trafficked area, he rounds on me, boxing me in against the wall. In an instant, it's like I'm back at his place on Earth all over again. The same reactions. The same fears. The same smells, even. His face has a few days worth of stubble, and a badly healed scar cuts across one cheek, stopping just short of his upper lip. His shoulders and biceps are bare, showing tanned, bulging muscles. He's nothing compared to Orri, but for guys down on Earth...

"Hey, I'm talking to you!" His grimy hand grabs my chin and forcefully turns it so that I'm looking right at him. He's so close now I can smell his rancid breath. My eyes dart past him, looking for any escape route. Any person I can flag down to get me the help I so desperately need. I could duck under his arms, and run like the wind, and...

"This was some stunt you pulled, you know that? But I can forgive you. You're mine, remember? And I'm here to take you home."

I nearly retch at the thought. "Adik..." I hate how weak my voice sounds. But when I'm with him, I'm defaulting back to my old behaviors. When I was with him I felt like a scared, trapped mouse. And even though I know better now, he still terrifies me. Reminds me of a time in my life I tried so hard to leave in the past. "We don't..." I shake my head and swallow around the building bile in my throat. "We don't have to do this. Let's not make a scene. We can go somewhere and talk. We —"

"Oh, we'll be talking all right. I expect you'll have *lots* to tell me." He emphasizes the word lots as he takes in my body from head to toe. His gaze makes my skin crawl. There's no way he could know about Orri or Bjornick...right?

"Stupid breeding agency," he mutters under his breath, spitting on the ground next to him. "If you wanted a baby that badly, you shoulda just asked me. You're pathetic. Running away to this glorified whorehouse so some alien asshole can do a pump and dump? You're even more of a slut than I thought. But that's all right." He yanks me closer, grabbing my hair and pulling so I'm looking straight up at him. "You might smell like alien ass right now, but I can change that. And whatever's in here..." He ghosts a hand over my belly, and it takes a moment to register his horrific intentions. "We'll take care of *that,* too."

The thought hits me why Orvox wanted to run the blood tests before I boarded the shuttle. It wasn't just to make sure I was healthy. She wanted to check if I was pregnant. And if I was...

The thought of a new life inside me brings forth a rush of fresh adrenaline, giving me the strength to fight through the panic. Not only for my sake, but for my baby's. I lunge to the side and twist my wrist like Orri showed me, using his momentum against him to break his grip. With a yell, he lets go for only an instant and I use that opening to bring my knee up, hoping to smash his balls as hard as I can.

He's too fast for me, though, and dodges the attack just in time. With a cry he grabs me again, this time even harder. He pulls me to him until I lose my balance and crash into his body, his face right next to my ear in a greasy whisper. "You'll stay quiet and come with me. You already know what happens if you don't listen, sweetheart." I shiver. I hate that name. "Looks like we need to make a little detour before heading back home."

I shiver again, but know better than to try and fight him. I'll never win on strength alone. I need a plan. And to do that, I'll need to play along, at least for the time being. So I bow my head, act like a good little omega, and get on the waiting hover bike. As we zoom away from the spaceport and down the roads leading to the wilderness, one thought lodges itself firmly in my heart:

I have to survive.

VENGEANCE

ORRI

I don't want to approach Isabella empty-handed. Especially after making such a fool of myself. But I don't know what will suit her fancy. Nothing seems good enough. Or it seems too trite, too gaudy to make for a proper gift.

Flowers, desserts, jewelry. Nothing catches my eye. It's customary to present one's mate with a gift to reveal one's intentions, but I never got to that point with Zannah. And now, with so much riding on this decision, I'm at a loss.

I am about to turn and leave the market when I hear a faint tinkling sound from one of the booths tucked away in the alley. I can't put my finger on it at first, but it sounds almost…familiar?

Then I recognize it: it's one of Isabella's favorite songs from Earth. She told me about a lullaby her mother used to sing to her when she had a nightmare and couldn't sleep. She told me how it always calmed her down and made her feel safe. She even played a copy of it for me on the network's video stream.

It's a soft, lilting tune, but full of emotion. Hope. Safety. Warmth.

All the things I hope I can be for Isabella in the future.

It's perfect.

I head over to the stand and interrupt the merchant standing there before he can even go into his sales pitch.

"I'd like one of your music boxes." I point at the one on the display. "One that plays that song."

The merchant nods, a bit taken aback by my abruptness. These merchants are used to having to haggle for every last credit, and here I was wanting to make a purchase outright. "Yes, yes!" He yelps, eyes alight at the prospect of a new sale. I have no idea how much these must cost, but with the exorbitant import fees on top of the materials and labor…

I grimace. My credit balance is gonna be feeling it later, but I have more than enough to treat Isabella to something special. She deserves it.

He scrambles and ducks under the table to pull out a beautifully wrapped red and gold gift box. "Very good gift." I notice he's not wearing a translator, leaving him to muddle through Aesirheim's language alone. Makes sense, though. Universal translators are incredibly expensive, and the ISA furnishes them as part of the contract between our planets; we need them in order to form relationships with our omegas. For everyone else? It can cost an arm and a leg — nearly literally.

The merchant makes a big show of winding up the example music box again. The song starts anew, a small dancing figure bobbing up and down among stars and clouds. "All the way from Earth, 100% authentic, guarantee!"

I know that if I don't close the deal as soon as possible, he'll try to sell me another dozen things. It's easier to sell to a warm lead, after all. But I've been a regular at the markets for years. I know how to deal with his type.

Pulling out my comm, I tap in a number that feels right and a slip of paper prints out, marked with my ID number and signature. I hand it across the table before he can think of any other ideas. What did Isabella say this thing reminded her of? A 'checkbook'?

"Will this be enough?"

The merchant looks like he's literally struck gold. His eyes bug out, his mouth drops open. "Yes, yes of course! Here, let me give you a special gift! Bonus!"

He puts another box on top of it, and a gilt-edged card as well. Putting them all into an elegant gift bag, he hands it across the stand. "Thank you for your business, sir! Do come back, we have many deals!"

I nod in thanks and hurry back to my mount. With my gift in hand, there's only one thing left to do.

Confront Isabella at last and tell her how I feel.

I PUSH my mount just a little faster, heart beating with the gravity of what I'm about to do. I've rehearsed what I'm going to say in my head a million times, but I'm sure once I see her again my mind will go blank.

There's no words that can really express how I feel, or why I did the things that I did. All I know is that my heart is full — full of love for Zannah, yes, but there's a new part there, just waiting to be completed.

My love for Isabella. And as I sink into the sway of my mount's hoofbeats, I know that's what it is. I was a fool to ever think otherwise. She's so soft, and small, and perfect, and —

Mine.

I know I royally screwed things up last time we saw each other, but I'm hoping she'll at least give me a chance to plead my case. If I can just talk to her, maybe I still have a chance. Because my heart knows what it wants now.

It wants her. *I* want her. In my life. In my home. In my bed.

Bearing my children. Being a mother, a wife, a family…

We're both a little broken, but when we're together it's like two disjointed puzzle pieces finally finding a match. She's good for me, and I was just too blind to see that before. Too prideful, too stubborn to see what was right in front of me.

When I return to the cottage Isabella and I had been staying at and find it empty, I fear the worst. I'm not surprised, though. Perhaps she's long gone by now. Perhaps she's found another mate already. I wouldn't blame her.

Holding on to a rapidly fraying thread of hope, I call up Orvox and wait as it rings again and again. Finally, her voice comes on the line.

"Is Isabella with you?" She's the first to speak, and her urgency does nothing to quell my rising fear.

"No…" I start. "Why? I thought she would be…"

A sigh. "Look. I'm not supposed to be telling you this, but we're at a bit of a loss here. I saw her just a few hours ago, we were running the final checks to clear her for re-assignment." My stomach sinks. *Re-assignment.* That meant…

"But here's the problem," Orvox continues. "I told her to meet me at the spaceport with her things, but she never showed. Her tracker's malfunctioning as well. I was about to call you up, hoping you knew something, but…" Her voice trails off.

"I'll find her." I'm interrupting before she's even done speaking, my heart in my throat as I think about her alone and defenseless in the wilds. "I've done it once before, I can do it again."

"Orri." Her voice is firmer this time. "I'm sorry, but this matter is out of your hands now. She's formally voided the contract, and any further involvement would be —“

“I said, I’ll find her.” I make no mistake of the determination in my voice, then close the voice line. With a cry, I put on a burst of speed, making a beeline for the spaceport and hoping I’m not too late.

* * *

HER SCENT HANGS in the air, ever so faint. I can’t place it, can’t track it. If only I knew what direction she’d gone. The dock fills with the roar of engines as the shuttle prepares for takeoff. I look at the monitor in a panic. She’s not on there, is she?!

But no. The scent isn’t coming from that direction. It’s faint, but palpable.

It doesn't smell like the soft, sweet scent of arousal or satisfaction I've come to associate with her, though.

It smells like pure fear.

An icy realization slithers through my veins. She wasn't missing because she wandered off and got lost. She was in danger.

Again.

I curse aloud, scanning the scene for any sign of her. Any evidence which way they had gone. I'd failed to protect her. Again. But I swore on everything I had, that this would be the last time. Once I got her in my arms and told her how I felt, she'd never have to feel afraid again.

Adrenaline pumps through my system, sharpening my senses. I look for anything out of place. Anything that doesn't belong.

Bingo. There's a duffel bag, stuffed haphazardly out of the way in some bushes next to the parking spots for the hover bikes. No doubt about it. It's hers.

And that means that some asshole does have her.

With murder in my veins, I whistle for my mount Alyx and hop onto her back, running after the faint trail at top speed. I'm not going to let her go through that pain again.

Whoever has her, he's going to die by my hand.

PLANNING AHEAD

ISABELLA

I wish I could say that I was used to getting kidnapped by now. It is the second time in such a short span, but this time it's almost worse because I know my captor. I fled the entire planet to get away from him, and here he is.

Never thought I'd have to face him again. Never even planned what I would do if I did. Brief, painful flashbacks haunt my memory, but I have to focus. I have to figure out where we're going.

And I have to figure out a way out of this one. Alone.

No highly-trained squadron of alpha warriors are coming to rescue me this time. No knight in shining armor is going to swoop in at the last minute. This is my battle to face, and I'm going to tackle it head on.

I'm no longer the scared little girl I was back then. I've gone through so much, and learned and become stronger because of it. I've trained with Orri, and faced my fears, and dammit, came to open my heart to someone even though I swore I never would again. I'm so much stronger now, and he just doesn't realize it yet. I can get my way out of this. I just have to make him think I'm going to be a weak pushover like I used to be, and then escape when I have the chance…

Pushing the panic to the side, I take in our surroundings as the hover bike speeds away from the space port and away from the cottages. He's heading for the mountains, away from the patrolled areas and toward the border of what Orri called the 'safe zone'.

Adik must have done his research. How he even got maps or information about Aesirheim is beyond me, not to mention how he got on the shuttle and found me here in the first place, but none of that matters right now. I try to think amidst the fog of fear and determination. The mountains.

Didn't Orri say something about a group of migrating creatures, just at the edge of the safe zone? I try to remember, but the facts all run together. I know from our talks that there are many different types of creatures here on Aesirheim, and not all of them are friendly. But these, a type of flying lizard called dactyls, look a lot scarier than they actually are.

"They're quite docile most of the time," he explained to me when we were walking near the lake. It seems like ages ago now. "But when their mating cycles come on — much like yours and mine — they get very aggressive. Very hostile toward anyone who might harm their young. Especially alphas like us."

I remember blushing at the time, but this little tidbit of information might be just the thing that will save my hide.

We come to a fork in the road. One side goes to the mountains. The other deeper into the forest. If we get stuck in the forest, it will be even harder for anyone to find us, but I know the dactyls like to nest in those trees.

If I can just trick him into going that way… "Adik," I speak up over the roar of the wind in my ears. "You don't want to go that way!" I point toward the forest instead of toward the mountains.

He snorts. "And why's that? You got your buddies waiting in ambush or something? I looked at the maps. I know what I'm doing. No way am I gonna stay out in the open there in the valley."

"No, I'm serious!" I try to sound as convincing as possible, reminding myself that my very life's on the line. "The forest's cursed!"

"Ha, I'm not going to fall for that." Adik sneers. "It's just a shortcut, that's all. Once we get through the forest and past the river, we'll be out of your little friends' borders. They can't touch us there."

"Adik, please!" I beg, and to my surprise real tears start to well up. "The mountains have huge cave systems. They talk about people getting lost there all the time. Wouldn't that be better if you wanted to hide me?"

"You talk too much." His grip tightens on my waist, so much that I can barely breathe. "We're going through the forest, and that's final."

As he turns the bike and we speed toward the forest, I go over the plan again in my mind.

Adik bursts through the forest on the hover bike. The dactyls take notice. They swarm Adik since he's the male and is causing the damage. Get back to the bike somehow. Make a run for it. And then... I haven't thought that far yet.

I just hope the dactyls are still there…

WARNED AWAY

ORRI

"Yeah, I got the feeds." Ulfar beeps me through the comm. If the ISA isn't going to help me on their own, I have other methods to try. "Cams show your girl getting on a hover bike with some human guy. Never seen him before. Had this weird striped tattoo down his left arm, but that's about all I can tell at this resolution."

My heart nearly stops. It can't be. "Repeat that," I say, voice shaking.

"A striped tattoo? It's not that uncommon, I guess. But all I got was the back of him, so I don't know what his face looks like. He's a piece of work, though, I can tell you that much. Listen — don't do anything stupid. The ISA's sending out a team. I already volunteered. We'll be on our way for backup, just…hold out till then."

I don't care if they send the entire army to save Isabella. I'm not waiting another second. Ulfar is still yapping in the background, but I tune him out as best I can.

"Kidnapping like that? Poor girl. Isabella, right? She's been through a lot already. Can't keep her out of trouble for even a second."

I growl at the mention of her name. I don't want anybody to malign my absent omega.

"I didn't mean anything by it, of course!" Ulfar scrambles to cover his tracks. "Just…why her? What's so special about her?"

"She's mine." And that's all he has to know. I click off the comm and let out a breath, fists clenching and unclenching. If my hunch is right, things are even worse than I imagined.

I remember when we were sharing our stories. Isabella told me about a man down on Earth that treated her badly. Made her afraid, even though he should have treated and protected her. She came to Aesirheim looking for a new life, and I swore up and down that if I ever came across the sorry sack of shit, he'd pay for ever hurting my omega.

My omega. The words felt somehow right in my heart. I just hoped that she saw it the same way.

If it really is that son of a bitch Adik…

I push Alyx faster, racing west. He won't live to see another sunrise.

WHEN I REACH the fork in the road leading to the forest or the mountains, I need to make a choice. If I pick wrong, it could mean the difference between life and death. I try to put myself in Adik's shoes. If I wanted to get away and hide somewhere I wouldn't be caught, where would I go?

My comm beeps again, interrupting my thinking. I don't want to answer it. However, when I see it's Ulfar, I groan and patch him through. "What now?"

"You're heading toward the border. Be careful. If he gets out of range, we won't be able pursue them without a permit from the neighboring lord, and —"

"Screw the permit!" I shout. "Wouldn't you have done the same thing for your sister?"

It's a low blow, but he doesn't realize just how serious I am about this.

"I...I'm sorry, man. Just be careful, okay? And remember the dactyl migration path goes right through there."

"Who?" I barely hear over the sound of my own heartbeat.

"The dactyls, remember? Soren sent out a memo to our entire team. We're supposed to stay away from them."

Shit. He's right.

"They won't take well to you barging in there guns blazing."

I grunt. Why now? I can't afford to get attacked by an overzealous monster or a pack of them while I'm trying to save Isabella. I don't even have my armor on, but I do have my weapon. I don't want to kill them, but if I have to...

"It's not worth it, man. They travel in packs, and I don't care who you are, you can't take on a whole herd of them alone. Wait for me at least—"

With a frustrated roar, I hang up the call. I'm not waiting for Ulfar to show up.

Isabella — who I now know is my real heart-mate — is worth fighting for. It's time for me to fight for my mate.

FOREST

ISABELLA

"So you really had nothing better to do on Earth, huh?"

"You crazy? I was worried sick about you. Why do you think I came all the way up here?"

I can think of a few reasons.

"How'd you get on the ship, anyway? When I went through, they had very specific rules about that kind of thing."

"I have my ways. If you thought this little whorehouse racket they have going on was gonna protect you, you don't know me very well." He turns the bike into a thicker patch of forest; I have to duck to keep from getting brained by a low hanging branch. "Come on Bella, you know I take care of what's mine."

My stomach churns. I hate the way he says mine. I hate the way he acts like this is normal, like I should be crawling back to him. Like he's the good guy and I'm just a misguided, lost little girl. Maybe at one point I would have believed that, but I'm a hell of a lot smarter now. Stronger, too.

And if I can keep him talking, that buys us more time for the ISA or Orri to find us.

I wish he hadn't swiped my tracker back at the spaceport. He was too fast, and I was still reeling from the shock of seeing him again. Orvox gave all of us one when we joined the program, and while it allowed them to track my movements, it also allowed me to call for help if things got out of hand. Now that I'm without it, they won't know where we are. All part of his sick plan.

There's no more panic button. If I am gonna get out of this one, I will have to do it myself.

Even though I'm scared for my life, Adik needs to know I'm not the same scared little girl I once was. I'm full of fire and determination, and part of my plan involves getting him worked up so he'll fall for the trap.

"Adik," I whine as annoyingly as possible. "I've gotta go to the bathroom. Think you can pull over?"

"And let your buddies catch up with us? Nice try. Now stop bothering me. Shut up and let me drive. We'll be out of here soon, and then we can finally be together. Won't that be nice?"

He's gone totally, utterly insane.

We tear through a curtain of low hanging vines. Some of them snag at my clothes and skin, leaving weird, slimy marks behind. Ugh. Gross. But Adik keeps driving, deeper and deeper into the forest. We left the path long ago and can barely even see where we are going. He's probably trying to take the shortest path possible to the border, no matter the cost.

"Pleeeease," I tug on his sleeve. "For meeeee."

The bike screeches to a stop in a small clearing; I lurch forward. Adik turns around, fury in his cold eyes, and slaps me, hard across the face. "I said shut up!"

I reel at the sudden pain, sucking in a breath as I bring a hand up to touch the reddening skin. Adik's seething, his flat palm now clenching into a fist...

Thump! A low, shuddering *crash* nearby makes us both freeze, and I thank my lucky stars it stills his hand. Something is moving nearby. It's coming closer. Could it be...?

Holding my breath, I try to remember what Orri told me about the dactyls.

That their appearance belies their generally soft, docile personality. That they'll do anything to protect their tribe, even attacking suspicious looking bystanders.

"But don't worry," he reassured me. I remember that much. "They only go for the men."

Trying to still the raucous beating in my chest, I take a deep breath and listen. There's the sound again. They're coming closer. Any minute now, they'll break through the brush...

"What's that?" Adik nods toward the sound. "You're the expert here, right? They gonna give us trouble?" He glares at me, eyes narrowed. "And I swear to God, if you lie to me—"

"Oh, it's nothing." I try to sound as casual as possible. "Just a herd of deer, probably. The rangers come out here to hunt for their pelts and meat." With a shrug, I go quiet.

"Well it sounds like it's our lucky day. I was getting hungry." He pulls out the blaster strapped to the side of the bike. My breath catches in my throat. I was so busy trying to look at the surroundings and make sure I could find my way back to safety that I hadn't noticed what he was packing on the bike. He had a gun, and that made things a *lot* more dangerous.

What if instead of his fist, he used the blaster next time...?

No. He wouldn't. I had to believe he had at least that much humanity left.

Time for a change of plan.

"You know," I start, looking at the blaster. I've seen some of the warriors carry them, but they tend toward more close-combat weapons. Something about wanting to look their enemy in the eye as they kill them. "A lot of the rangers around here don't even take weapons on these hunts. The deer are big, but they're so docile any man worth his salt can take down one with his bare hands."

Adik sputters for a moment. With a growl, he holsters the weapon. "What are you trying to say?"

"Oh, nothing," I say sweetly. "Just that if you were a real man, you'd take down one of those deer for me and make me a nice dinner. Or do you not think you can do it?" I flutter my eyelashes at him. I know I'm laying it on thick, but he has to buy my story or the whole plan's foiled.

"I can do it!" Adik scoffs. "Just who do you think I am? Some stupid alien deer isn't gonna stop me."

"Good. Then I'll just watch over the bike while you —"

He grabs my wrist, hard. "Not so fast. You think I'm really gonna leave you alone? Not a chance. You're coming with me." Adik yanks me off the bike; I stumble to regain my balance. "And if I find out you're not telling the truth...well. We wouldn't want that."

Even though I'm more scared than I've ever been in my life, I press my lips together and play the part. I bow my head and go with him, each step leading me closer to my doom...or my salvation.

The die was cast. We were heading right for them.

Hopefully Orri's intel was right about the dactyls not attacking women...

Oh, Orri. My broken heart cries out to him in my time of need. I was a fool to push him away, not after everything he'd done for me. We could have made it work, if both of us had gotten our heads out of our asses. But now I don't even know if I'll have a chance to see him again.

Or Lara. Or Janie.

Or my unnamed baby.

As we hike deeper into the forest and toward the crashing sounds of huge hooves, I sent out my most desperate plea:

Orri...where are you?

TRAP

ISABELLA

The footsteps are growing louder. I can smell their scent in the air. It's just as Orri described it. A distinct, earthy smell with an undercurrent of spice to it. Almost like getting black pepper up your nose, now that I think of it. Except this scent doesn't make me sneeze.

It does, however, make my heart beat even faster. We're getting closer to their tracks, and if they see Adik dragging me around, who knows what they'll do...

"Come on, keep up." Adik growls, yanking on my wrist so hard it hurts. I stumble over the uneven ground, panting and scratched and just hoping that this is the boon I so desperately need.

There's another sound in the gloom. A high pitched, warbling cry. It sends a chill down my spine. Do dactyls make that sound? In the heat of the moment, I can't remember anything anymore. Adik pulls me to a stop, eyes searching. "What was that?" He rounds on me. "Did you lure us into a trap or something?"

I twist my arm away now that we're standing still, rubbing the sore skin there. "No," I say without meeting his eyes. "It's probably just a bird or something."

Adik grumbles. "I don't like it. On second thought, I'm not that hungry anyway. We're wasting time." He turns. "We're going back to the hover bike. Now."

No! Not when we're this close!

"Don't tell me you're scared." It's a risky taunt, but one I have to take. If he turns away now, my plans along with any hope for rescue will go up in smoke.

I was with Adik for long enough to know his patterns. He, and every other man on planet earth it seems like, despises one thing above all others — someone questioning their courage or masculinity. It's a low blow, but one I know he'll respond to.

"What did you say?" He hisses.

"No, it's fine." I shrug and put up my hands. "I get it. You heard a sound and got scared. We can go back to the bike where it's safe."

"You little..." There's that fist again, and this time for sure I'm gonna get hit, until...

There's that screech again. Louder. Longer. And like something from Jurassic Park, this creature crashes through the underbrush and straight toward us!

"The fuck! This ain't no fuckin' deer!" Adik yells, clamoring for the gun at his side. I doubt he's ever used one a day in his life, just wanted it to look cool. And it's that moment of hesitation that costs him everything. The dactyl, in all its huge, fierce glory, head butts right into him, sending him and the gun flying.

I make a lunge for the weapon, but no sooner have I moved than a second beast crashes onto the scene, letting out the same warbling scream. Was that their battle cry? Were they going to attack me too?

I roll out of the way just in time, but the clawed foot of the beast comes down hard on the blaster, shattering it into useless pieces. There goes our only weapon. Pushing myself off my butt and back onto my feet, I look around for anything I can use in the meantime. Something big, something heavy, I don't care...

A fallen branch about as big around as my arm and three feet long catches my eye. Still watching the dactyls out of the corner of my eye, I make a beeline for the branch and pick it up, brandishing it in both hands. I feel like some kind of caveman, but if the creatures — or Adik, for that matter, decide to turn on me, I'll be able to defend myself.

Or at least bonk them silly and buy enough time to run back to the hover bike.

Speaking of Adik, I scan the scene. He's laid out against a tree, looking stunned but still conscious. A trickle of blood drips from a gash at his temple, and he looks more wild, more feral than I've ever seen him. Pushing himself onto his feet, he lunges past the charging dactyl just in time. With a thud that shakes the whole forest, the poor animal ends up head butting the tree trunk at full force, leaving it wobbling and dazed on its feet.

Then he sees me, and his face is nothing but murderous fury.

"You bitch!" He grunts, running right at me. "You knew about this, didn't you? You set me up! You're going to pay for this!"

Fight or flight kicks in. My grip tightens on the branch. I have one shot to make this count. I don't want to hurt him, but I don't have a choice. Just as I'm winding up, about to take the swing of my life, one lands right in front of me, rearing up on its back legs with a scream. It's not attacking me. In fact, quite the opposite.

Is it...protecting me?

I don't have time to think. Only to act. With the dactyl between us as a distraction, I bolt out of the way, past Adik and toward the trees. For a moment, I can hardly believe myself. Only a few short months ago I would have never even dreamed of doing something like this. I was far too timid. Far too naive and hooked on my own powerlessness.

Now, I have the strength to choose my own fate.

"Good riddance," I mutter under my breath, as I turn and run for the bike. More dactyls pour out from the trees. The whole herd's approaching now, riled up by the violence. I had no idea there were so many of them. Their cries echo in my ears. Their thundering footsteps shake the already uneven ground. The world spins but still I stumble forward, tripping over what feels like every root and rock. I pick myself up and keep running. I can't look back.

To look back is death. To look back is to leave that chapter — that part of myself and my life — wide open. No. I'm closing that book. I'm moving forward.

The bike comes into view at last, but the dactyls are coming in all directions. They're screeching and tearing at the ground and oh god, there's so many of them. I can't get through! Razor-sharp talons lash out as one takes a giant leap, and I throw my hands up instinctively to defend myself, sure that this is the end...

And then I hear the loudest, most startling, and most welcome sound I've ever heard in my life.

It's Orri, barreling toward us with a war-cry that makes even me quiver in sheer intimidation and awe. It drowns out the roar of the creatures closing in around me, and only one thought remains.

He's here. He came.

I am full of warmth. Maybe he hasn't given up on me after all.

TERRITORIAL CREATURES

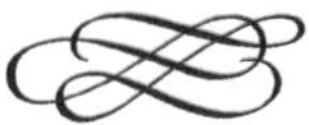

ORRI

The roar of the approaching dactyls fills my ears. Dread, then realization, then even more dread washes over me as I push my mount faster, faster than I've ever gone before.

She'd been listening to me, after all.

The dactyl migrations were still in progress close to the border, and they were very territorial creatures. Which meant that if Isabella and her captor were to run across them...

They wouldn't go after her. She wasn't a threat. If they did, it would go against everything we knew about them. But hey, I've been surprised before. So I clench my jaw, let out a shout of determination, and tear into the forest.

My heart pounds with every gallop of the beast beneath me. It swells with something I've never felt before, a kind of internal connection that leads me, largely by instinct, toward my missing mate.

The smell of her drifts on the air. It's her all right, there's something different about it. I can't put my finger on what, so I push it away. Keep riding. Keep moving forward.

Orri... I hear her voice in the back of my mind, plain as day. She's nowhere to be seen and yet I heard her as clearly as if she were standing next to me.

Was this what Soren and Rathgar were talking about? Was this the true heart-mate connection so fabled and rare among our peoples?

Maybe this was what I'd been looking for all this time. What I'd been too afraid to let myself have until now. Love. Companionship. A beautiful, wonderful woman that means the world to me.

I realize now that it doesn't undo the memories I have with Zannah to move on with my life. I will forever miss her, but living my life to the fullest and grabbing onto whatever happiness I can is what she would have wanted.

At last, I realize, that's the true way to honor her memory. Not by living in shame, but by living without reservations. By putting my heart and soul into everything I do, just like Zannah did. It's probably just the rush of emotions or the heat of the moment, but I can almost hear her voice too, whispering to me that it will be alright. That she's proud of me.

And maybe that's just the closure I needed.

Isabella! I call out in my mind. I have no idea if she can hear me, but I just hope she knows I'm on my way...

And I hope I won't be too late.

I BURST into the clearing when I see the herd stampeding into a frenzy. I pull my mount to a skidding stop and try to survey the situation, but there's just so many of them. I could take down a few, maybe even a dozen if I was lucky, but this many? I'd be overwhelmed in no time. I'm not wearing any armor, and not only do they have numbers on their side, they have razor-sharp talons that can cut through a man's skin like butter.

I'm standing there, trying to calculate my options, when I see a small figure fleeing just in front of them. I hadn't noticed it before when I was trying to count the number of dactyls in the stampede, but I would know that scent — that gait — those flowing locks of hair anywhere.

It's her! But she's not alone — and I'm not talking about the screeching stampede that surrounds us. There, only a few strides behind, is the shape of a man, bloody and limping, but with such pure hatred in his eyes I know what's happened at once.

Everything clicks together in a fraction of a second. The man. The very same man Isabella told me about from her past. It's him. The vile, worthless creature she'd called Adik.

And the very man I swore to destroy with my own two hands if I ever crossed paths with him.

Looks like it's my lucky day.

Something snaps within me. The part of myself I always try to keep controlled — the raw, alpha mentality that permeates my very being — smashes through every shred of rationality I have left.

I let out a bone-shaking roar straight from my chest. The world narrows and slows. All my senses hone in on Isabella...and the snarling man running after her. The dactyls don't matter anymore. I'll take a million scratches from their talons if it means keeping Isabella safe.

And if it means finally ridding the world of that pathetic excuse for a lifeform.

Adik. A fitting name for *a dick.* The word tastes like poison on my tongue. As the gods are my witness, he will not see the dawn.

The sound of my war-cry doesn't have an affect on the dactyls, but it's loud enough to startle Isabella and Adik. She looks up, sees me heading toward her, and her face lights up with unthinkable relief. I want to remember that gaze of awe for the rest of my life. I'll be the best damn mate she's ever had, but first, it's time to take out the trash.

Isabella changes directions, running away from the hover bike I now see stashed among the trees to the east and toward me instead. This sudden change, however, catches her off balance. She loses her footing with a cry and I'm already rushing toward her as fast as I can when I see her ankle twist and her body fall toward the ground in slow motion.

It's then that I realize the instinctual way that she cradles her belly as she falls, almost as if...

Another surge of adrenaline and power and fury shakes the forest as I cry out her name. It all comes together at last. The subtle change in her scent. The way I can feel her calling out to me, even from so far away. The crazed look in her attacker's eyes. And the way she holds her stomach, as if protecting something within.

She's pregnant!

I leap off my mount still in motion, flying toward Adik with my sword raised. Consumed with bloodlust, all I can think about is ripping his head from his body. Spilling his guts upon the ground and showing him the true power of an Aesirheim alpha.

He's lunging toward my mate, but I'm faster. He doesn't know what's hit him as I slam into his body and knock him to the ground. Stunned, he stares up at me with glassy eyes. "Who the fuck are you?" He groans, still trying to lean around me to get to Isabella. The dactyls screech and swarm around us, coming in for the kill.

I grab his greasy hair, yank his head back, and press my blade to his pale throat before leaning over to speak into his bleeding ear.

"Her mate, you son of a bitch." And with that, I make one simple slicing motion, and it's done. He gurgles, clutching helplessly at his throat, and collapses to the ground.

The beasts are all around me, screeching and baring their talons, but when I move away from Adik's body and sheath my weapon, holding up my hands to show I mean them no harm, they flow around me like water. They're going straight for something — no, someone — else.

And the last thing I see before I turn away and rush to Isabella's side is Adik's broken corpse being brutally picked apart by a writhing mass of monsters. A fitting end.

Another second and Isabella's in my arms, sobbing and trembling, but she's here and she's mine and there's nowhere else in the world I'd rather be. I press a kiss to her forehead. Run my hands through her hair. Relish in the warmth of her body. She's here. She's real. She's alive.

My heart's still hammering a mile a minute, my brain still trapped in the horrible panic of potentially losing her. Flashbacks of Zannah's last moments flicker into reality, and the fact that I came so close to losing yet another woman takes my breath away.

But I didn't. She's safe. And I vow, right there and then, that I'll never let anything happen to her again.

"Shhh," I soothe, brushing the tears away from her face. She buries her head in my chest, fingers clutching desperately at anything they can reach. "I'm here now. I'm here."

"You..." She sniffles loudly before looking up at me with wide, reddened eyes. "You came back. I thought..."

"I was a fool. I was too scared to see what was in front of me."

"But..."

"No buts." I shush her with a kiss. "Not anymore." I let out a breath. "What I'm saying is...will you still give me a chance? Can we start over?"

She chokes out a half-sob, half-laugh, and even in her terrified state a small smile begins to creep up her face.

Another rush of energy surges through me, not just through my heart but down my spine and to the tips of my fingers and toes. At last I understand.

"You're my heart-mate, Isabella. And I never want you to feel alone or unsafe again." I nuzzle into her hair and draw in the scent. It's soft and perfect and beautiful, just like her. "Will you have me?"

Isabella trembles in my arms as I stand, still carrying her. We walk back to my waiting mount and as I help her onto its back, she sways with exhaustion and shock. One thing is for sure, however. The way she leans into me as I hop onto the beast behind her. The way she covers my hands with her own.

"I will," she says softly. Sleepily. "Thank you...for believing in me."

And as she melts into my embrace, we set off toward the surrogacy center. Together.

COMFORT

ISABELLA

For the first time in what feels like forever, I'm not injured, endangered, captive, or in heat. As Orri and I ride away from the scene and back onto the trails toward the surrogacy center, I feel nothing but a calm, exhausted sense of relief.

I guess I don't have the energy left to feel anything else. That had been a close one. Far, far too close. Even though Orri came to my rescue at the end, I'm still proud of my quick thinking. I'm proud of myself for finally standing up to Adik once and for all, and even though the thought of him being devoured by monsters makes me a little queasy to my stomach, I know he brought it upon himself.

There's a sense of lightness in my heart and in my gut, knowing that he won't be able to bother me anymore. I wouldn't say that I'm glad that he's dead, but it feels like I can finally breathe. Like I can stop looking over my shoulder and finally move on with my life. Speaking of which...

"How did you know where to find me?" I murmur. My head lolls against his warm, strong chest. His wide hands hold me against him as we ride.

The mount bobs up and down with a steady, soothing motion that makes my eyelids heavy. Much more of this, and I'll fall asleep right here in his arms.

"I put two and two together. We'd been tracking their movements, and when I saw your bag back at the spaceport I thought the worst. But then I got a call from my colleague Ulfar, and when I realized you were heading right toward their migration path..." I craned my neck to face him as he rubbed the back of his neck. "I gotta admit, I thought it was all going in one ear and out the other when I was going on about the field reports the other day. But you remembered, and you used that knowledge to buy yourself time. That was really smart thinking. Couldn't have done it better myself."

I'm silent for a moment, my mouth opening in awe until it curls up into a smile. Orri, the fabled alpha warrior, was proud of *me*? "I didn't do much," I shrugged, my cheeks red. "I only remembered a little, but I knew I couldn't take him down myself, so I had to find something that could."

His hands run up and down my back protectively. He purrs the words in my ear, making me squirm. "You were so brave back there, Isabella. And I'm so proud of you for facing the dactyls alone like that. Even we usually don't approach them without backup."

My heart swells with pride at the thought.

Orri clears his throat. "I was actually, um, hoping to find you for a different reason. Before I realized you were gone, that is."

"Oh?" That part I hadn't expected. It seems so long ago now, that fateful argument that split us in two. What made him change his mind?

"I had a little chat with one of my colleagues. He also happens to be a very good friend. Or was." Orri pauses, shifting in the saddle. "He's also Zannah's brother."

"What happened?"

Orri snorts. "Let's just say he made me realize how blind I was." He shakes his head and pulls me closer. "He reminded me of what's really important."

"And what's that?" I think I know what he's talking about, but I still want to hear him say it.

"Not giving up on things — or people — that mean the world to me." He lowers his head to kiss the nape of my neck. "And that just because I lost someone doesn't mean I'm never allowed to feel happy again. He made me realize that I can have both."

At his words, the pieces fall into place. Something shifts and clicks inside of me, as well. The feelings for Bjornick I had were real. No, they *are* real. He'll always have a special place in my heart. But that doesn't undo or minimize the way I feel about Orri, either. We've both been through so much. We both have our baggage and our broken hearts, but when we're together, it feels like maybe there's hope for me after all.

And as he describes his conversation with Ulfar, I realize that maybe this is just what I needed as well. Closure. Permission. And the comfort of knowing that wherever he is now, that Bjornick would look down on me and smile, for having the bravery and the heart to continue to chase my dreams.

I lean back into him, smiling and letting my eyes flutter closed. For the first time in what feels like forever, I'm at peace. I'm safe. And I don't know where life will lead me next, but I know that I want to have Orri by my side.

He presses his face into my hair, scenting me deeply and letting out a deep groan. I can't blame him — even without the influence of the hormones, the scent of him makes me feel sleepy and sexy all at the same time. But then he tenses against me, sniffing again. Deeper. His arms tighten around me and my heart skips a beat.

Did I smell or something? Roughing it through the jungle and nearly getting trampled by a dactyl herd wasn't exactly the cleanest thing I'd ever done. But no, there wasn't a look of disgust on his face. It was almost...awe?

"Your scent," Orri rumbles, his voice deep and husky in a way that makes my toes curl. "It's different. Are you..."

And then I realize what he's talking about. When Adik first said something about it, I thought maybe he was trying to play with my head. Make me afraid, even if there was nothing there. But as his fingers intertwine with mine and I place his hand over my belly, both of us feel a strange shock. Like touching metal and feeling a spark, the touch of my mate's hand upon my belly triggers something within me.

It's early — much too early — to be feeling anything down there, but I swear I can feel a flutter, deep down inside. A greeting, almost. A preview of what's to come.

"I don't know for sure," I say breathlessly, my voice cracking. "I didn't think anything about it and then Adik said something, and it all made sense..." My voice trails off. That feels so very far away now. Was that what they'd been trying to check on the lab tests at the center? There was only one way to find out.

"Fuck." Orri grunts, holding me tighter than ever. He digs his heels into the side of his mount and we pick up speed, the air rushing through my dark hair and sending it flying out behind me in loose waves.

"Is that a good thing?" I venture. Thought after thought piles into my mind. When I signed up for the surrogacy program, I knew it involved having a baby, but at the time that was no more than an abstract concept. A means to an end to get me off planet and to a safe haven, far away from my abuser.

So much had changed since then. Now that the possibility was here in front of me, I found the idea...exhilarating.

No, I realize as we bound toward the center. More than that. With Orri here at my side, the soft pink glow of sunset, and the tall grasses swaying around us, it feels *right*. No longer do I have to worry about looking over my shoulder. No longer do I have to wonder what if, to watch others live their lives as mine passes me by.

I have a mate, and a home, and a family. And soon...if all goes according to plan...the blessing of a child.

"It's a very good thing," Orri promises me, kissing and nipping at the sides of my neck and my ears. I squirm and gasp against him as the village draws back into view. "You're coming home with me, Isabella. For good this time."

As I relax into his embrace and let the fear and stress fade away into a calm, comfortable peace, I know there's nowhere I'd rather be.

COOKING

ORRI

A FEW DAYS LATER

The sun's not even up yet, and I'm bustling around the kitchen making breakfast. Who am I, and what have I done with the old Orri? I smile to myself as I reach into the fridge and pull out the milk and juice.

I never cared much for cooking when it was just me, but now I have someone to cook for. After I got Isabella home and rested, we had her checked out by both the ISA and my clan's doctor. They both confirmed what we knew in our hearts already: she was pregnant. The real shocker was what they told us after the checkup — that they detected not one fetus, but *two*.

Twins. I can't believe it. As I flip the sizzling bacon and put a few more slices of bread in the toaster, I can't keep the smile from my face. How did I ever get so lucky?

At that thought, I hear movement behind me and turn to find Isabella standing in the doorway, dressed in my robe. It's way too large on her and the belt's only loosely tied, giving me an eyeful of what she has on underneath. Namely — nothing. I nearly drop the frying pan and take in the sight of her.

Messy bed hair, half-open eyes, and my robe draped loosely around her soft, curvy flesh. My mouth waters at the sight. Maybe I'm hungry for something else, after all. She yawns and stretches while rubbing her eyes and taking in the spread of food before her. "What's all this?" She mutters, leaning against the door frame. "Since when are you so into breakfast?"

I look up just long enough to catch the way her eyes light up at the sight. I could get used to that. "Since the doctors told us you need to rest up and eat up. Gotta get your iron levels back to normal, remember? That's why you were having those dizzy spells."

She just yawns again, nodding. "You try carrying two little people inside of you. It gets tiring."

The thought still sends a shiver down my spine. I still can't believe it. Not only did I get the girl, but she's going to have not one, but two babies. I'm nervous, of course — all the military training in the world can't prepare me for looking after a little one, let alone two — but I'm also excited to start this new part of my life.

For so long, I watched other couples and thought I'd never be able to have what they had. That the opportunity had passed for me long ago, and there was nothing left for me but blood and battle. But finding Isabella and opening my heart to her changed all of that. I realized that I still had plenty of life to live. And I realized that continuing to deny myself out of some misguided sense of loyalty was only keeping me stuck in the past.

Now, I have a beautiful woman by my side. An Earth woman, in fact. Definitely never thought I'd end up with a human, but surprisingly, it works. She's soft and sweet in all the right ways, and firm and feisty where it counts.

She's been watching me train every morning since we returned together. I know she wants to participate, but her body's still adapting to the pregnancy. Instead, I let her use a recording device and film each of my workouts.

It serves a double purpose — it will serve as training material for the new recruits, of course, but let's just say we made a couple of private videos for her eyes only. She'll have plenty to keep her occupied while I'm out on patrol, and I even got reassigned to a unit closer to home so I can watch over her.

All in all, things are looking up, and for the first time since Zannah passed away, I find myself actually looking forward to the future.

"I'm just one person, you know." Isabella laughs, joining me at the counter. She wraps her arms around my midsection and hugs me from behind. "How am I supposed to eat all of this?"

"I'm just following the doctor's orders. You've got to get your iron up, plus you're eating for three, remember?" I try to make it sound like that's the only reason. Not because I love taking care of her like this. It's the alpha nature in me coming out, now that we've accepted one another as mates.

Being an alpha isn't all about being a growly sex-crazed animal, after all. Of course, that's a part...a very sexy part, I think with a smile. But even more important than that is the way that alphas treasure and protect their mates.

Being with Isabella like this is more than I ever expected. More than I ever thought I deserved, especially after Zannah. But when I'm with Isabella, she makes me feel like a king. And I'm going to do everything in my power to spoil her like the treasure she is.

Gotta admit, I could get used to this.

She looks past me at the table and sees a full breakfast spread. She nudges me playfully. "For someone who claims not to like cooking, you sure does a good job of it."

Pancakes, fruit, yogurt...I tried to remember all of her favorite Earth foods and put them together for her. It took no small amount of shopping and watching videos on Earth cooking techniques, but I think my efforts are finally paying off.

Bacon sizzles in the pan, letting off the most mouth-watering aroma. Toast dings in the toaster, ready to be spread with the delicious green-colored jam that is a local specialty.

Everything is seemingly...somehow...perfect.

Maybe that's not the right word. If there's one thing I've learned from my trials, it's that life will never be perfect. There will always be things you don't expect, heartbreaks you couldn't see coming, and pains that seem utterly all-consuming. But in the midst of it all, there's joy and hope and community and *love*.

And that's something worth fighting for.

"Go sit down." I shoo her away with the spatula. "I'm almost done, and then we can eat. Besides, I have a surprise for you."

She perks up. "A surprise? What are you talking about."

"You'll see in a minute. Now shoo." A few more waggles of the spatula later and she relents, stepping around me back into the dining room. I sneak a peek at her backside as she leaves — humans really are just built different. I'm a lucky man.

Speaking of which...

After checking that Isabella's situated at the table, I duck into the pantry and pull out the box I've been saving for this moment. It's the music box I bought at the market that day. I never had a chance to give it to her because when I was on my way, I found out that she'd gone missing.

I may not have a ring, but I have this. And in some way, that makes it even more meaningful. As I hold the box in my hands, my heart starts racing all over again. We're not even in danger this time, but my hands are sweating. My mouth goes dry.

Since when did this human affect me so much more than all the life-or-death battles I've been in? Clearing my throat, I let out a deep breath and step into the dining room.

She's looking up at me, eyes full of life and hope and not a little amount of anticipation. That's one of the things I love about human eyes — they're so expressive. So much more so than Aesirheim women. "So?" She says in that cute, lilting voice of hers. "What's this surprise you're talking about?"

A last minute idea pops into my mind and I run with it. "Close your eyes."

"Wha—"

"Trust me. You'll see what I mean in just a moment. Just close your eyes. I'll tell you when to open them."

"Okay." Her lids flutter closed and she sits there, hands folded in her lap, waiting.

As gently as possible, I pull out the box and place it upon the table. It makes a soft click as I turn the key, and as the first notes spill out, I move to behind her chair and place my hands on her shoulders. "Open your eyes."

And there it is. A tinkling lullaby all the way from Earth, played across the backdrop of a beautiful mechanical music box. She claps a hand over her mouth, eyes widening in shock and recognition.

"Orri..." She gasps, still staring. "Oh my god...you..." Tears well up in her eyes, but they're not tears of pain or fear. Not ever again, if I have anything to say about it. Isabella rips her eyes away from the music box to look up at me, mouth agape and eyes shining with tears. "How did you..."

Thank you, Ulfar, for the tip. Definitely gonna have to buy him a drink after this.

"I found it at the market," I say, rubbing the back of my neck. I had hoped that she would be excited, but I wasn't prepared for this level of reaction. "I remember you talking about a song you grew up with, and when I was doing some shopping the other day I heard it, and it reminded me of you." That's only a half-truth, but she doesn't need to know that.

"It's beautiful," she says, practically sobbing at this point. "Thank you." Isabella turns in the chair and wraps her arms around me, burying her face in my shirt.

While part of me hates to see her crying, I know it's the release from so much stress and trauma in so little time. Perhaps it's the catharsis she needs to move forward with her life. I went through the same thing when I realized that Isabella was it for me.

When Ulfar, Zannah's brother, finally gave me the permission I needed to move on.

So I hold her, stroking a hand through her hair, and think about all that we've been through together. All of the new memories that we can share, and the family we're going to build.

I tip her chin up and press a gentle kiss to her soft lips. I trace the tracks of her tears. I lean in close and whisper through her hair—

"Isabella, will you be mine? Forever?"

She clings even more tightly, and when I meet her eyes again, they're filled with nothing but love. I see reflected in them all of the hurts and all of the struggles, but all of the laughs and joys and dreams. "I would love to," she says, voice breaking at last.

As the last few notes of the music box warble across the room, a different sound catches my attention.

Grrrr.

Oh, right. The food. Sounds like someone's hungry.

We both break into easy laughter, and I rush back into the kitchen to fix her a plate for breakfast. I hope this is the start of many happy mornings to come.

EPILOGUE I: BIRTH

ORRI

My heavily pregnant wife is in the infirmary, ready to give birth to our hybrid children. The future of our family is at the delicate point between being held safely in her womb and entering the hard world of Aesirheim. I clench my fists, uncomfortable with a challenge I cannot face with strength or power. As the father of our twins, I can only wait uselessly while my heart-mate gives birth.

I pace outside of the room that they won't let me in, saying that birth is a time for women to surround her. Lara, Iris, and Janie already came by to give Isabella gifts for the twins. Those gifts are sitting on a table in the room. I can see what is happening through the glass windows, but I am extremely restless. Isabella told me that on Earth, fathers tend to be in the room when mothers give birth. Here on Aesirheim, the healers have decided to keep me out of the room. They think that I'm too impulsive.

I have to distract myself. Isabella told me that on Earth, there's a tradition of asking men to boil water. We don't have traditions like that on Aesirheim.

When we started losing the babies inside of our own females, birth became a sacred ritual. The healers carefully oversee every bit of development of the fetuses inside of our females' wombs. Isabella has rolled her eyes about how many check-ups she has had to have over the course of pregnancy, but she signed the contract to bear my child. It turned out that she's going to bear my children.

"Hey," Soren says, coming in and hitting me on the shoulder. "How do you feel?"

"There's nothing for me to fight." There is a fear inside of me, which has lived there for the entirety of Isabella's pregnancy, that she'd lose our twins, just as many female Aesir who were not omegas had lost their children.

"I know what it's like. My own wife said that I should distract you." Soren grins.

"How?" I am ready to be distracted.

"Let's go train. Your comm will bring you here when she has gone through the last stage of human labor."

I looked through the window at my wife. There are warring emotions inside of me. On one hand, I want my wife to know that I'm here. However, she's in so much pain that I don't think she'll notice if I slip out. They haven't let me go in and hold her hand.

I go outside with Soren to the nearest training ground. He tosses me one of the blunted weapons we use for practice. I look at the dull edge, meant for the greenest of warriors. Without warning me at all, he attacks.

Finally, my mind is able to stop worrying about my pregnant wife. As I attack and counter-attack, Soren's face contorts. He gives a battle cry and picks up the pace.

I guess that his wife thought he needed the exercise before she sent him over. From the way we're both breathing hard, it seems like his decision to use practice weapons was a good one. When he uses a heavy overhand strike, I lift my weapon to block him over my head. At that moment, my comm lights up.

"Please come to the infirmary," a cool robotic voice says.

I step back and bow to Soren, ending our practice bout. I throw the practice weapon at him, knowing that he'll take care of it. Warriors always take care of their weapons.

And fathers always take care of their children on Aesirheim. I run back to the infirmary, breathless when I arrive. "How is she?" I ask the nearest healer, who is finally letting me into her room.

"She's just fine. We're weighing your children right now."

I rush towards the bed, where she has raised her arms. She's sweaty and exhausted, but there's a lot of satisfaction in her dark eyes.

"My heart-mate," I tell her, "how do you feel?"

"Tired. Happy." She puckers up, so I kiss her mouth, measuring her emotional state. She's really happy and joyous right now.

"Orri? We've cleaned up your twins. Do you want to hold them?"

I spin on my heel, looking at the babies swaddled in blankets.

"Go sit on the chair in the corner, Father," one of the healers says, laughing. "We'll put one in each arm."

I follow her order and sit on a chair in the corner. The healers bring my newborn children right to me. Both of them have their eyes closed. One yawns, and the other one is clearly asleep.

The first time I touch them and look into their faces, warmth spills in my chest. I don't know if I have ever felt anything as profound as holding my children. As an alpha, I thought that I might never have a child. Plenty of us don't.

"You are a miracle," I tell my family, looking at how happy Isabella is right now; she is turned towards us but still on the bed. "All of you."

The healers steal my progeny away and put them in clear cribs so that we can still see them. I get to my feet and surge towards my wife, kissing her again. "Sleep now, my love."

Her mouth opens, but she falls asleep before she can reply. The healers tuck her blankets around her and motion for me to sit back in the chair in the corner. When I sit down and look at my three family members in that room, I feel like the luckiest Aesir on the planet. Who could ever want more?

Silently, I promise them all that I'd protect and provide for them. When Soren mated his omega, I had no idea I'd ever get to experience having my own family. I understood why his wife had sent him to stand watch with me. It was hard to explain what it was like to become a parent to an alpha without children.

EPILOGUE II: FIRST BIRTHDAY

ISABELLA

"We're running late," I comment to my child, Leo. He responds by chewing on the ends of my hair. I gently remove the hair from his mouth, which just revs up his desire for more. I plop him into one of the baby carriers that the Aesir have, one that looks somewhat like an automated bouncer back on Earth.

"Lyra? Sweetheart, where are you?" I call.

Soon, I hear a coo coming from around the corner. She has been suspiciously quiet for the last few minutes. I pray that she hasn't done anything too terrible.

When I come around the corner, hoping that Leo doesn't get up to shenanigans, I see that she is playing with building blocks. They are precariously placed, and the entire structure is about to fall down on her. To keep her safe, I scoop her up in my arms. She screams in defiance, deeply offended that I would dare interrupt her playtime.

"Both of you need to get dressed for your first birthday party," I chide.

They have no idea what the day means, but I do. The Aesir have a tradition of celebrating a baby's first 100 days and first year of life. They had so many stillbirths and problems with their young that it is a miracle to them that they have babies at all.

As a result, my husband has gone a bit over the top for this celebration. All of his comrades have been invited, even though not that many alphas have been mated to humans. I can see some longing on the faces of a few of his colleagues; I know that they'd like to pay for contracts themselves. Of course, the fees are only one part. Genetically matching doesn't happen for most people immediately.

Absently, I hum, thinking about what might have been. The babies sing along with me, wordlessly. They can make sounds, but they haven't conversed with us yet. I'm glad that they are teething on schedule.

"Hello, heart-mate," Orri says. He's grinning at me as I spin with Lyra in my arms. In two strides, the two of us are in his embrace.

Immediately, Leo complains about being left out. Orri chuckles and lets go of us.

"And who is my big boy?" he asks our son. Leo laughs as Orri tickles his armpits and tummy. There is a special bond between Orri and his first-born son. One day, he can learn to be a warrior just like his father. He already has plenty of honorary uncles who have given him miniature weapons as teething toys. The first time it happened, I was alarmed by the idea of our son choking on one of them, but Orri assured me that all of the Aesir boys received the same gifts as soon as they born. Our daughter had been given other toys, since the Aesir jealously protected their females. They'd have to adjust to how Earth females believed in gender parity, which was an ongoing culture clash. Orri had already taken plenty of heat for teaching me how to fight; I fully expected him to train Lyra by Leo's side and treat them the same way. Zannah had been a warrior, after all, before her death. It seems like a way to honor her memory.

As I watch Orri play with our son, I feel warmth in the depths of my soul.

Who knew that signing a single contract would have had such a happy ending?

I turn to my husband. "Can you help me get the children changed for their party?" Orri hired an event planner for the entire party, due to how many people he had invited. It was a serious thing to celebrate your children here on Aesirheim.

Thinking about how things could have been, I shiver. I would never have been so secure if Adik had successfully married me and kept me with him through our shared children on famine-stricken Earth. Even though neither of us Earthlings had understood how dangerous dactyls were, I am still grateful that Orri's commander had sent over reports about staying away from their migration route. Without them, I wouldn't be here.

"Of course, my heart-mate," Orri responds. He kisses my hair before sweeping Lyra away with Leo. I go into our closet to put on the silk dress that he wants me to wear today. It is embroidered with the dactyls that saved my life and prevented Adik from traumatizing me on Aesirheim.

I put on the loose pants that come up to my natural waist. I never wore them on Earth, but it is part of becoming an Aesir by marriage. The other Earthlings and I helped design slightly more comfortable versions for ourselves, especially since we're always carrying around our children. They are so cherished on Aesirheim that it's hard sometimes to remember how difficult it is to care for children back on Earth.

I pull my hair back with one of their hair adornments. For my children's birthday, I look like a true Aesir wife. My children have a golden tone to their skin, like their father. Because the agency brought multiple women over at the same time, we have a little friend group. We can all pitch in and help out with all of the new babies, but it hardly seems like an onerous burden when almost of the Aesir are crazy about babies. They train their children to tell their parents about everything they need with sign language before they can talk, so we don't hear a lot of wails from our very spoiled children.

After I watch Orri care for with our children, I feel warmth in the depths of my soul. Who knew that signing a single contract would have had such a happy ending?

Orri comes back into our room with our children in his arms. They are wearing silk, too, but the Aesir are practical enough to put a bib over the silk, which is cleaned by technology that the Aesir consider commonplace. We put them into a double stroller perfect for our kiddos. Orri whispers into his comm that we are coming; the event planner is in charge of making sure everyone feels welcome.

When we go into the event center that Orri rented out for this party, I can see that the party is already in full swing. The warriors are all drinking ruou, the local booze, and the women are with the kids in one corner. There's a buffet with all kinds of Aesir food prepared for all of our guests. Our event planner has coordinated everything perfectly. It's not a formal event where we need to shake hands with people in a receiving line. Instead, the kids are playing with each other.

A clump of the male Aesir is watching training bouts that are already over on a giant screen in one corner. Some of the young boys and girls are lingering near the warriors without bothering them, which would make their mothers whisk them away. One day, Leo will be one of those boys. Maybe Lyra will want to train like her brother will, but there are more options for her; it seems that the Aesir are hard in order to hold onto their respective territories, and my child is being raised somewhat like a boy in Sparta of Ancient Greece. My hope is that our children will grow up happy and safe. When I look at the room full of people who love them, I think they have a bright future on Aesirheim.

EPILOGUE III: ANOTHER BIRTH

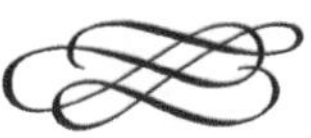

ORRI

OVER ONE AND A HALF YEARS LATER

"Hey man, you really need to calm down. I'm sure she'll be fine."

Ulfar is at my side, saying something that's supposed to be helpful, but I barely hear him. Doesn't he understand that my mate is in *labor*?

"I know," I pout, pacing the waiting room for the umpteenth time. "But what if—"

Ulfar holds up a hand. "I'm gonna have to stop you there. Listen. I know it's our job to look for weaknesses and prepare for every eventuality, but Isabella is in good hands. The doctors will take care of her, you just need to trust that." He meets my gaze, and his expression is caring, but serious. "Last time she had twins and was a-okay after some bedrest. This should be easy by comparison."

I let out a heavy sigh. He's right, of course he's right, but my omega in labor dials up every protective instinct to eleven. It's probably a good thing I can't hear her from here, or I'd burst into the room before I could stop myself, and they'd have to escort me out. Again.

Learned *that* the hard way last time.

"Where are the twins, anyway?" Ulfar asks. "Usually you're attached at the hip."

I smile at that. Before I met Isabella, kids were only an abstract idea, so far on the horizon that it was practically invisible. Nothing could have prepared me for the chaos that is raising twins, but I find that I'm enjoying it a lot more than I thought I would.

"Leo and Lyra are spending the day with Rathgar and Janie. Rathgar's not gonna admit it, but I think he just wants another little one to dote on. He was practically begging me to let him watch them."

Ulfar chuckles. "You got that right. Here, let me get you something to drink. Anything in particular?"

"Coffee," I say without missing a beat. "Black."

Only a minute later, Ulfar presses a cup of scalding hot coffee into my hands. The temperature catches me off guard and I hiss, nearly spilling even more over my bare skin.

"Careful," I groan. "You know I'm a mess right now."

Ulfar rolls his eyes, but there's mirth behind his expression. "You alphas, I swear. You go all bonkers over this stuff. I don't get it."

"You're an alpha, too," I grunt. "Or did you forget that?"

Ulfar shrugs. "Eh, it's never been an important part of my life. I'm pretty happy as it is. Don't see why chasing after a woman would make things any better. After I watched you mope after Zannah died, there's not a lot of appeal."

I snort into my coffee. "That's what they all say."

"Oh, come on. Not you too." Ulfar shakes his head at me.

Barking out a laugh, I finally plop down into one of the hard chairs and throw my arms over the backs of the surrounding ones. "I'm telling you, man. It's different. You think you know what's gonna happen and then boom."

"If you say so," Ulfar chuckles. "I'm just getting all the enjoyment I can out of watching you all acting like fools." He meets my eyes. It's clear that he wants to continue to give me a hard time about how worried I am about my wife.

My mind's still racing and my thoughts are all over the place, but I know Ulfar's tactic. He's trying to keep me engaged so I don't worry about Isabella. And it's working.

Mostly.

We banter on like that for a few minutes more, sharing old stories and gossiping about new ones. When I finish my coffee and take our cups to the cleaning station, an idea pops into my head.

"I just thought of something," I say after returning.

"What, you left the stove on at home?"

I give him a playful swat against the back of his head and he cringes, groaning out a choked laugh. "No, you dummy. I finally figured out how I was gonna get you back for making fun of me 'freaking out' over Isabella."

"Oh?" Ulfar raises an eyebrow. "And how's that?"

"Bet when you're in my shoes, you'll be just as much of a wreck. Or more." My lips curl up into a grin. Ulfar may be my superior in a professional context, but he's still one of my closest friends.

Ulfar scoffs. "That's hardly a bet. No magic omega hormones are gonna change me *that* much. Besides, I've been in the system for years and nothing's come of it. If I was gonna be genetically matched, they would have done so already."

"Oh, so you don't think you can do it?" I know it'll get a rise out of him, and the more I'm bickering with Ulfar, the less time I'm beside myself with worry.

"I didn't say that!" Ulfar sputters. "I just think it's all kinda—" He waves his hand, looking for the words—

Ping!

Ulfar's comm device goes off and he furrows his brow, hand ghosting toward his belt.

"You expecting a call or something?"

"No..." Ulfar starts. "That's why it's weird. I don't have this thing connected to any of the networks, either. It's probably just a—"

As he looks at the screen, I can visibly see the color drain from his face. His mouth drops open. Immediately, my brain jumps into battle mode. Was something wrong? Were we being attacked? An emergency meeting with Soren, perhaps?

Ulfar looks up from the device like he's just seen a ghost. "Speak of the devil," he breathes. "I just got a match."

"You what?!"

But before I can find out anything more, the swinging doors open and a woman's calling my name.

"Orri? Is there an Orri, mate of Isabella here?"

"Me!" I shout a little too loudly. I jump out of the chair, all thoughts of Ulfar's impending match a distant memory. "What's wrong? Is she okay?"

The nurse nods with a smile. "Of course. She's delivered a healthy baby boy. You can go in and see if you like."

The world narrows to just that moment. My heart leaps into my throat, blood rushing in my ears. I push past the nurse, down the endless corridor, and right into the room marked with her name.

And there she is. A sweaty, exhausted Isabella holding a swaddled bundle against her chest. Her eyes tell the real story — that despite the immense physical strain, she couldn't be happier. She's practically glowing as I slow my steps and approach our new son for the first time.

"Isabella," I breathe, looking down at the newborn and then back to her. "He's..."

"Beautiful," she finishes, her eyes brimming with happy tears. "Our new son."

The whole world seems to shift on its axis at that moment. My heart, already full with the love and acceptance I never knew I needed, swells even further. The rush of battle is nothing compared to this. A pure, thoughtless high that I want to remember forever.

I reach out and touch the red, heated skin of our new child. Looking at his impossibly tiny fingers and toes. Of his small, slightly parted mouth. And at the tiny tuft of dark hair covering his head.

Words fail me. All the past, present, and future fade away in the light of this singular, shining moment.

I have the love of a beautiful woman, three children, and a life that I wouldn't trade for the world. I never thought I'd end up here. I'd resigned myself to a life of solitude and grief. But Isabella smashed into my life the day I saw her in that cell, and she taught me things about myself I'd long since buried. She helped me learn to live again.

Somehow, somewhere, I know Zannah, and all those who came before her, would be proud.

www.ingramcontent.com/pod-product-compliance
Lightning Source LLC
Chambersburg PA
CBHW030604310726
48979CB00003B/568